MURDA MITTEN

BY

RENITA M. WALKER

Rocky D Publishing, LLC
www.rockydpublishing.com

Also by Renita M. Walker

Like Night & Day

What's Done in the Dark

Ain't No Sunshine

Thick Like Water

Sara & Smooth

Promiscuous Girl (the full length novel)

Murda Mitten in the anthology *Bitch I'm From the D*

Promiscuous Girl in the anthology *Soak N Wet*

Like Em Low in the anthology *Hot N Bothered*

Rocky D Publishing, LLC
P.O. Box 85214
Westland, MI 48185

This book is a work of fiction. Names, characters, places and incidents are either products of the author's imagination or used fictitiously. Any resemblance to actual events or locales or persons, living or dead, is entirely coincidental.

If you have purchased this book with a dull or missing cover — you have possibly purchased an unauthorized or stolen book. Please immediately contact the publisher advising where, when and how you purchased this book.

Copyright © 2009 by Renita M. Walker. All rights reserved. No part of this book may be reproduced in any form without permission from the publisher, except by a reviewer who may quote brief passages to be printed in a newspaper or magazine.

Library of Congress Control Number: 2009911856
ISBN: 9780984328031
Author: Renita M. Walker
Cover Design: Marion Designs
Typesetting: HDB Editorial Services
Editor: HDB Editorial Services / hdbeditorialservices@yahoo.com
First Trade Paperback Edition Printing February 2010

10 9 8 7 6 5 4 3 2 1

Printed in the United States of America

DEDICATION

I dedicate this book to all of those who have lost a family member or friend to violence in the city of Detroit.

In no way am I trying to glorify or condone violence. I too have lost family and many, many friends to the streets of Detroit. At one point in my life I thought I would become a statistic like many of my peers. I am blessed to be able to use my imagination to do what I love to do while entertaining others in the process. That's just what this is… entertainment. I hope you are thoroughly entertained.

CHAPTER 1

Bo woke up feeling hot and sticky. This summer had been one of the hottest she'd ever experienced in her twenty-six years of life. She was grateful it was Saturday because that meant a lighter workload. Bo worked seven days a week, but refused to see more than three clients on Saturdays and Sundays. Although throughout the week it wasn't uncommon for her to see five or six clients in one day.

"Ahhhhhhhhhhh," she said out loud as she stretched out her arms before hopping out of bed and walking over to turn her computer on. She had to check her schedule to confirm which three clients she needed to see today. She also had an appointment to get her hair and nails done then later she would meet up with Chris—her friend with benefits—for what she was sure would be a much-needed drink.

Bonita was what most would call "cute." She was 5' 5", 130 pounds and was a caramel complexion. When her long black hair wasn't up in her customary ponytail, she wore it in big, bouncy curls that reached the middle of her back. She was well proportioned with her 34C breast, 26-inch waist, and an ass that looked like it belonged on a thicker girl. However, Bo had never been a conceited girl, if anything, she was very modest.

Once she got her internet up, she glanced at the headlines before clicking the button to pull up the Excel spreadsheet showing her client list. One headline in particular caught her eye and she quickly minimized the spreadsheet so she could read the story.

The results are in; Detroit is the number one crime capital of the United States. The State of Michigan has been termed the "Murder Mitten" due to its shape and frequency of murders in cities like Detroit....

Reading the news story made Bo even more determined to fulfill the promise she'd made herself a year and a half ago, after the murder of her best friend, Krystal. She'd promised herself in two years time she would save up enough money to move out of Detroit and pursue her dream of writing a novel. Her goal was to make a million dollars before hopping in her silver 2008 Mercedes C300 Sport Sedan and hitting the road. The only thing she planned on taking from her apartment was her computer. The other things would be replaced when she started her new life. She wanted nothing to remind her of the life she was leaving behind.

Going back to her spreadsheet she saw she had three clients to see today—Rahiem, Rochelle and Tre'. After printing a copy of her schedule, she turned off the computer and began choosing the outfit she would wear now and another outfit she would change into tonight before meeting with Chris. After settling on a pair of True Religion jeans and matching wife-beater to wear now, she grabbed a sexy, white, silk, tube mini-dress to wear out tonight. Next she grabbed a pair of cute Gucci flip-flops that matched the purse she carried yesterday as well as the matching shoes and purse she would wear with the dress. Bo headed to the shower hoping all would go well for her today.

Thirty minutes later, Bo was inconspicuously parked on a side street in a crowded Southfield neighborhood. It was a spot she'd gotten very familiar with over the last few days as she began the preliminary work with her client, Rahiem. It was only nine thirty-six in the morning, yet residents were coming and going like it was lunchtime or something. That was the reason Bo felt comfortable staking out her client's home in this manner. Typically, she would never chance being spotted; but in this neighborhood full of working husbands and soccer moms, and cars coming and going, carpoolers waiting for their occupants were commonplace.

After sitting for another five minutes, she saw her client exit his front door and head over to the driver's side door of his dark cherry metallic 2008 Chevy Trailblazer SS parked in the driveway. Bo looked at the young man as he retrieved what looked like an empty backpack and a silver motorcycle helmet from the truck and made his way back into the house. He was tall, about 6' 4". He had a solid chocolate body, from what she could see through the sagging jean shorts and white tee he was wearing. He finished off his thug look with white Air Force Ones, a white fitted hat, and a platinum chain with a diamond cross on it; that was blinging so much Bo could see the sparkle from the fifty feet separating them.

Moments later, Bo heard the hum of a motorcycle before seeing Rahiem shoot out the driveway and fly right past her. Shortly after, she took off behind him, and he led her to I696 East. After riding for about twenty minutes, they exited I696 at Gratiot and made a left. Bo made sure to stay a safe distance behind Rahiem so he wouldn't notice her trailing him. Once he turned into a shopping plaza parking lot and pulled into a parking space, Bo followed suit and parked where she could keep an eye on him, hoping she didn't have to follow him through the stores.

Bo's prayers were answered when a few moments later a white 2007 Tahoe pulled up next to Rahiem and parked. Bo watched as Rahiem jumped off his motorcycle and took his helmet off before hopping in the front passenger seat of the Tahoe. It was hard to see what was going on inside the truck due to the dark tinted windows. Before Bo's curiosity got the best of her, Rahiem hopped out the truck and continued talking to the driver. Bo smiled when she noticed a much larger bulge in Rahiem's backpack.

As the Tahoe backed out the parking space and headed out the parking lot, Rahiem put his helmet back on and hopped back on his bike. Bo slowly began to exit her parking space and headed over to Rahiem. She had no idea how this would pan out, but knew it may be her only opportunity to catch Rahiem alone.

Bo's timing was perfect. Just as Rahiem eased out of his parking space, Bo came flying up his lane. Frozen in fear, there was nothing Rahiem could do to prevent being hit. His thoughts were consumed by the $49,500 he'd just exchanged for three keys. He gripped the bike tighter, closed his eyes, and braced himself for the hit he was sure to come. Seconds later, Rahiem opened his eyes just in time to see the silver Mercedes screech to a halt to prevent hitting him.

"Oh my God! I am sooo sorry! Are you all right?" Bo asked, laying it on thick as she exited the car and ran over to Rahiem. "I was so busy thinking about getting to Ruby Tuesdays that I wasn't paying attention to my speed."

Rahiem's initial anger was replaced by lust when he saw the beauty in the Benz approaching him. His first thought had been to slap the shit out of the bitch, but once he realized he could see her fat ass poking out even as she walked towards him, thoughts of slapping her were replaced with thoughts of fucking the shit out of her. He could feel his dick start to rise as he removed his helmet and started to get off the bike.

"Are you okay?" Bo asked again.

"I don't know… let's move over there so these cars can park," Rahiem replied, pointing at the line of cars that were trying to get down the isle.

"Okay, I'll follow you." Bo made her way back to her car. She made sure to put a little twist in her hips because she knew he was watching. *This is going to be easier than I thought,* she thought.

Rahiem continued to watch as Bo got in her car. Once he heard a horn blow—indicating he needed to get the hell out the way—he replaced his helmet and headed over to a less crowded area of the parking lot. After parking, they stood outside Bo's car talking until Rahiem suggested they grab a bite to eat at the Ruby Tuesdays that also sat in the parking lot. Bo agreed and they headed over to park at Ruby Tuesdays.

The restaurant didn't open for another fifteen minutes, so they sat outside and talked while waiting. Bo didn't say much about herself; instead she let Rahiem run his mouth talking about his favorite subject—himself. During that time Bo found out Rahiem was a twenty-year-old balla who was originally from Ohio. He claimed to be single with no children. He also bragged about owning his own home, as well as a truck, car, and motorcycle. In actuality he did own his motorcycle, but the truck was a lease, the car was a used Honda he'd purchased at the auction for his baby momma, and he lived with his mom.

After being seated and placing their orders, Rahiem continued to brag about how much money he had. He was trying his best to impress Bo. She played the role and acted like what he was saying was really interesting, but her mind was focused on the task at hand.

"Let's keep it real, baby," said Rahiem, grabbing Bo's hand as it rested on the table. "I think you are sexy as hell, and I want you." Rahiem stared into Bo's eyes, waiting to see her reaction. Her eyes held no clues, so he was praying he hadn't fucked up. After clearing his throat he continued. "No disrespect, but I think we should leave here and hit a room. I don't be tricking and shit, but I got whatever you want."

Bo laughed inside as she listened to Rahiem run his weak game. "So you don't usually trick, but I'm the exception?" she asked.

"Naw, baby… you ain't no trick. This ain't gon' be no one-time thing. I wanna see you on a regular basis. I got you, baby—"

"Let's go," Bo cut him off. "I'll follow you." Bo began to gather her things.

"Right now! You don't want to eat first?"

"Nope, I want you right now." Bo licked her lips seductively.

Rahiem scrambled to gather his keys and backpack as he stood up from the table. He quickly reached into his pocket, making sure to pull out his entire knot for Bo to see then placed two twenties on the table. "That's what I'm talking about. Damn, baby. We gon' get along just fine."

Bo smiled as they exited the restaurant. *Yeah, this is going to be too damn easy,* she thought as she made her way over to her car. Once inside, she looked in her purse to make sure she had everything that would be needed. After confirming everything was there, she carefully backed out the parking space and began to follow Rahiem up Gratiot.

Once inside the room, Rahiem immediately grabbed Bo up into a tight embrace, gripping her ass. She used that opportunity to wrap her arms around his back, feeling what she was sure to be keys of cocaine in his backpack. As if he could tell what she was doing, Rahiem quickly pulled away from her.

"Let me take this shit off, baby," he said, removing the backpack and tossing it in a corner on the floor. "Take all that shit off. I'm 'bout to fuck you real good. Damn!"

"Wait a minute," Bo interjected just as Rahiem started to pull her shirt over her head. "You need to take a shower first."

"I just took a shower, baby. I'm straight." Rahiem stopped his attempt to undress Bo and began removing his own clothes. After getting down to his boxers, he noticed Bo was still fully dressed. "What's the holdup, baby?"

"I don't do stuff like this. I'm nervous, Rahiem. Just give me a minute. Let me use the bathroom right quick." Bo played it off.

Bo was smart. She'd stayed in her car while Rahiem paid for the room. Once he'd given her the room number and jumped on his bike to drive around to the back of the hotel where the room was located, she left her car parked and walked around to the room. She was used to being inconspicuous in her line of work. She was now sitting in the bathroom screwing the custom made silencer on her Sig Sauer P226.

"Damn, baby. What you in there doing? I know you ain't got yo' period or no stupid shit like that," Rahiem shouted as he removed his boxers and sat naked at the foot of the bed.

"No." Bo flushed the toilet to disguise any noise she may have been making. "I'm coming now… just give me a minute."

"Well bring yo' ass on," Rahiem mumbled under his breath. *I got other shit to do, bitch. Yo' pussy better be worth all the bullshit you putting me through, or I'm gon' kick yo' ass after I fuck the shit outta you,* he thought. The bathroom door opened, breaking his thoughts. "Well it's about time, baby. Now take all that shit—" The sight of Bo's gun pointed at his chest caused him to stop talking mid-sentence.

"Don't fuckin' move," Bo said in a low, even tone. "One move... and I'm going to blow yo' shit off."

"What the fuck is going on? What... you robbing me? Who the fuck put you up to this shit?" asked Rahiem.

"No, I'm not robbing you. I was paid to terminate yo' ass. You've pissed somebody off, Rahiem. So much so... they want yo' ass six feet deep."

"Bitch, what the fuck is you talking about?" Rahiem was about to stand when he saw Bo's grip tighten on the gun. He quickly sat back down. "You don't have to do this."

Bo stood at the end of the bed with her P226 pointing at Rahiem's chest. "You wanna know who killed you?" she asked. It was a question she asked all her clients before taking their lives.

"What difference would it make?" asked Rahiem while looking her in the eyes.

"Umm..." Bo stammered. "I guess it wouldn't make any. No one has ever asked me that. They usually just say yes, or continue to beg for their life."

Rahiem thought for a moment. There had to be a way he could get out of this situation. He silently cursed himself for once again allowing a woman to fuck him up. This time it seemed would be the last. "I'm just really amazed someone as beautiful as you can kill an innocent person with no remorse. Why do you do this?" Rahiem was trying to buy more time to think of a way to get the gun without getting himself killed.

"Fuck the Dr. Phil bullshit. I guess you don't want to know." Bo prepared to complete the job so she wouldn't be late for her hair and nail appointment at two o'clock.

"YES!" Rahiem blurted out, seeing that Bo was about to pull the trigger. "I want to know who put the hit on me!"

"Ya boy, Tony, the nigga whose bitch you fucking." Subconsciously she glanced down to see what Rahiem was working with. She was impressed with the eight limp inches resting in his lap.

"You gotta be fuckin' kiddin' me! I'm about to die over a bitch! A bitch that I don't even give a fuck about! I'll pay you double what that nigga giving you to reverse the hit. I'm a real ass nigga, baby. Tony is a sucka ass nigga. Let's work something out, baby. Damn, if I had a down ass bitch like you by my side we could take over the D... and you sexy as hell... just thinking about that shit making my dick hard. At least let a nigga get up in some pussy before—"

Bo glanced down to see more than ten inches of hard dick pointing straight up, poking Rahiem in his chest damn near. She cut him off, "That's very tempting, but once I kill you I'm taking that backpack you've been riding with all morning. I'm sure there's at least $20,000 in there. So technically, I'll be getting the $10,000 Tony paid me, plus whatever's in the bag. I can go get fucked once I leave here."

Before Rahiem could say a word, Bo shot him in the forehead. The force from the bullet entering caused him to fall straight back onto the bed with his dick pointing towards the ceiling. Bo grabbed the backpack and headed out the door, using the bottom of her shirt to place around the doorknob before opening the door. "One down, two more to go, and I can chill out for the rest of the day," she said as she walked to her car.

CHAPTER 2

"Damn, nigga... you 'bout to make me late for my hair appointment. Don't make me fuck you up," Bo joked with Quincy. At the sound of her phone ringing she looked and saw a 555 number she didn't recognize. *Probably a new customer,* she thought, ignoring the call.

"Oh, don't tell me I'm on yo' list," Quincy joked back.

Quincy was her best friend Krystal's brother and probably the only person she really trusted. He knew of her plans to leave the D after stacking a million. He also knew how she was making her money and often would send her customers as well as clients.

Quincy was one of the biggest dope dealers in the D. It was actually him who turned Bo on to becoming a hit woman. He'd suggested it in a joking manner and was surprised when Bo agreed with the idea. He was also the person who would purchase all the dope Bo retrieved during her hits—at a very, discounted price.

Standing at 6' 5" and a muscular 265 pounds, Quincy was what most women would consider fine as hell. He was a chocolate brown complexion and had eyes exactly like Young Jeezy's. He kept his head shaved and sported a goatee. Based on the size of his hands and his size fifteen shoes, a woman could only imagine what he was working with.

"Never," Bo said seriously. "Don't even say no shit like that, Q."

"Girl, I know you got my back... and I got yours. I actually got two more niggas I need you to make disappear by the end of next week."

"Damn, Q... you stay beefed out! Just let me know the details and I got you. But I still need $30,000 for these three keys, nigga. You can take this shit now, and I'll hook up with you later to get the details on the hits and my $50,000."

"$50,000! For what?" Quincy played dumb.

"$20,000 for the two hits and $30,000 for these three keys, nigga. Don't play dumb, Q."

"Okay... I got you." Quincy laughed. He enjoyed messing with Bo. He secretly held deep feelings for Bo and wished he could wife her. She was the person closest to his sister Krystal, whom his heart ached for every day. But he knew he and Bo could never be a couple, because she looked at him like a brother.

After a brief hug, Bo left Quincy's stash spot and headed toward the beauty shop. Her plan was to get her hair and nails done then head over to the dope house her next client ran. She was hoping to catch her client leaving the spot, follow her, and catch her slipping. Her plan was a long shot, because she knew she couldn't stake out the dope house without being noticed by one of the workers. She was hoping luck was on her side and she would catch her client leaving the spot.

All eyes were on Bo as she entered the beauty shop. Salon Extreme was known as the best salon in Detroit. All the ballas sent their girls there to get their hair and nails done. It was really out of Bo's character to frequent a salon such as this one, but her stylist of fifteen years had just changed salons and now rented a booth at Salon Extreme.

"Hey, Bonita!" her stylist Kim shouted from the back of the salon. "You're early, girl. I need about thirty minutes before I'll get to you."

"I know… maybe Kayla can start on my nails while I wait," suggested Bo. Just as Bo started to make her way over to Kayla's station she heard a loud commotion over by the receptionist booth.

"Bitch, I run the D! Ain't no bitches gettin' it like I'm gettin' it! You seen the 760Li parked in the alley… its meee… bitches!" a young girl yelled in the face of an older lady working as the receptionist in the salon.

The young girl was about 5' 3" with a small frame. Her hair was cut like Halle Barry's in *Swordfish*. She had on a red Prada baby-T with tight coochie cutter jean shorts. She complimented her look with all Prada accessories—purse, belt and shoes. She also had huge diamond studs in her ears, a diamond bracelet on her arm and a diamond chain with an iced out Hello Kitty emblem stopping at her belly button.

"I'm sorry," the receptionist said timidly, pulling her glasses up on her nose.

"Yeah, you are sorry, bitch! Questioning me about how the fuck I spend my paper! Yeah, I come in this bitch twice a week and spend $300! So what, I got it like that, bitch! It's nothing! And here's another hundred you can tip my stylist with, bitch!" She reached in her Prada bag and pulled out a hundred dollar bill. "You the mutha fucka making minimum wage at forty; I'm a ballin' bitch at twenty-two!" The young girl threw the additional hundred dollar bill in the receptionist's face before spinning on her Prada heels and walking toward the exit.

Bo could not believe her luck. The loud mouth girl was Rochelle—her next client. As Rochelle sashayed toward the exit she looked at Bo and rolled her eyes. Bo followed behind her.

"I left my cell phone in the car, and I'm waiting on a call," Bo yelled back to Kim. "I'll be right back."

"Okay," Kim replied while curling her customer's hair.

"These bitches better recognized," Rochelle continued to talk shit as she exited. She purposely let the door go once she made her exit, allowing it to close in Bo's face.

This one is actually going to be fun, Bo thought as she lagged behind Rochelle as if she too were going to her car. Her heart was racing as she spontaneously constructed a plan to get Rochelle.

"Wow! That's your car? It's beautiful," Bo said as they approached the alley where Rochelle's gold BMW 760Li sat parked under a light post.

Rochelle was a cocky, evil, bitch, but she loved for someone to ride her dick, so she ate the compliment up. "Yeah, that's how ballin' bitches roll. When you grow up maybe you'll be able to get you one. Naaa… you probably won't ever ride this good," Rochelle taunted Bo before chuckling.

Yeah, this is definitely going to be fun, Bo thought as she surveyed the area to make sure no one could see them. Once she saw it was clear, she pulled her gun from her purse and rushed to get closer to Rochelle, who had just clicked the alarm to unlock the doors and was reaching for the door handle.

"Get the fuck in and climb yo' ass over to the passenger seat you loud mouth bitch!"

Rochelle spun around with her face screwed up, shocked by the change in the tone of Bo's voice and how close she was up on her. "Bi—" was all she got out before shutting up after noticing the P226 pointed at her stomach. She stood there stunned, not knowing what to do.

Bo could see in Rochelle's eyes she was about to try her. Without many options, she quickly slapped her over the head with the gun, causing Rochelle to hit the ground.

Bo quickly opened the back door and dragged Rochelle into the car before any of the blood from the gash in her forehead could hit the ground.

Once Rochelle was in the back seat, Bo quickly pistol whipped her until she blacked out. Bo picked the keys up from the ground and jumped in the driver's seat. She grabbed the duct tape from her purse and reached in the back to tape up Rochelle's wrist and ankles. She also put a piece of tape over Rochelle's mouth.

Bo looked around cautiously to make sure no one had seen what just happened. Once she was confident no one had seen her, she slowly pulled out the alley and on to the side street.

"Now what the fuck I'm gon' do with this bitch," Bo said out loud. "This was stupid! This bitch got this hot ass car that anybody who knows her is going to spot." Although the car had tinted windows, Bo was hoping no one rode up on her thinking she was Rochelle. "I gotta figure out where I can dump this bitch without being seen in broad daylight."

Bo cautiously made her way to I96 heading east. She was already irritated, and the sound of both her business and personal phones ringing was beginning to drive her crazy. She glanced at the screen on her business phone and saw the same 555 number that had been blowing up her phone since earlier. She quickly answered her personal phone after seeing it was Chris calling.

"Bonita!" he said before she had a chance to say hello. "What are your plans for tonight, sweetheart?"

"Hey, Chris... I thought I was supposed to be going out with you tonight. Why? What's up?"

"Just making sure you didn't forget about me, sweetheart. I can't wait to see you. Wear something sexy so my co-workers will all be jealous." Chris laughed.

"Okay, where are we going?" asked Bonita.

"We are all meeting up at some spot downtown. I'll call you back with the details or you could meet me at the office and ride with me. Hey, what are you wearing right now?" he asked sounding freaky.

"I could be wearing nothing and lying across your desk." Bo was still horny as hell from her encounter with Rahiem.

"Damn! I'd love for you to make that happen, Bonita."

"I'll be there in an hour."

"Bonita... I love you."

"Okay... I'll see you soon, Chris." Bo quickly ended the call.

She hated Chris ended every call by telling her he loved her. Although she did *like* Chris, she promised herself just like De Niro said in the movie *Heat,* she would never allow herself to get close to anything she couldn't turn her back on and leave in thirty seconds if the heat was coming her way. She refused to go out like De Niro did in the movie and had stuck to her motto.

Getting back to the task at hand, she contemplated where she could find a secluded spot to dump the car with Rochelle's body inside of it. Once again, her personal phone rang, interrupting her thoughts. This time it was Quincy calling.

"Hey, Bo... I'm gon' need you to handle that for me sooner than I thought. You think you can do it in the next two days?"

"Q, you know I like to take a few days to watch my clients. What's your rush?" Just then the perfect spot to dump Rochelle came to Bo's mind. "Never mind, Q, I got you. I need a big favor right now though. I'm in the middle of something, and I need you to pick me up from Dexter and the Boulevard... like right now."

"Right now! I'm about thirty minutes away from there, Bo. And I'm on my way to handle some busi—"

"Fuck all that, Q… I need you. Can you pick me up or not?"

"I'm on my way… and Bo… be safe, okay?"

"I always am, Q. See you in a few." Bo ended the call and headed toward Dexter and Whitney.

Her plan was to pull up in the driveway of one of the depleted houses on the block, kill Rochelle and walk to Dexter and the Boulevard to meet up with Q. She glanced in the back seat to see a terrified Rochelle with eyes as big as saucers. Tears flowed from her eyes as she struggled to release her hands from the grip of the duct tape.

"Oh, you finally woke up. I know you ain't back there struggling, bitch." Bo chuckled. "You was a bad bitch back at the shop… cussing people out and shit. I can only imagine what's going through yo' head right now, but I can tell you one thing for certain. You are about to die. There is nothing you can do to stop that from happening."

Hearing this, Rochelle struggled to sit up in her seat, but stopped as soon as she saw the gun Bo pointed in her face.

"Now, you do have a choice." Bo noticed a glimmer of hope in Rochelle's eyes when she glanced in the backseat once again. "You can die without knowing who put a hit out on you, or you can die knowing the mutha fucka who caused this to happen to you."

Tears once again rushed to escape Rochelle's eyes. *I can't believe I let this stupid bitch catch me slippin'. Who the fuck put a hit out on me? Damn! This some fucked up shit. I gotta think of something to do,* Rochelle thought as she looked around to see if she could determine where they were at. But from the angle she was lying at she could only see the sky and an eighteen wheeler rolling past. Feeling a sense of lost hope, Rochelle slowly shook her head up and down, indicating she would like to know who put the hit on her.

"All of this could have been prevented if you would have just paid Gooch the $75,000 you owe him for those five kilos he fronted you three weeks ago. Now didn't he tell you that you had two weeks to give him his money? You should have listened, Rochelle," Bo said mockingly.

Upon hearing the cause of all this, Rochelle felt a sense of relief. She had called Gooch from the shop to let him know she had his money and could meet him to drop it off. However, she got his voicemail and had to leave a message. The $75,000 was in a Gucci duffle bag in the trunk. Now she only had to figure out a way to communicate this to the bitch that had pistol whipped, carjacked, and kidnapped her. *No matter what happens I'm still gonna kill this bitch and Gooch once I get this money to him,* Rochelle naively thought. She didn't have a clue who she was dealing with.

"What you trying to tell me?" Bo asked after looking in the back to see Rochelle desperately nodding her head toward the back of the seat. She was lifting her arms and pointing her hands towards the trunk of the car. "Are you trying to tell me that Gooch's money is in the trunk?" Rochelle quickly nodded yes. "Okay, we straight then," Bo bluffed. "Just let me find somewhere discreet to make sure you're not lying to me."

Rochelle released a loud sigh of relief. All she could think about was how she was going to get back at this bitch and Gooch. The speed of the car let Rochelle know she was now riding in a residential area. After a few turns, the brightness from outside disappeared.

Bo was unable to find a spot on Whitney because there were a few people outside. With a stoke of luck she'd turned down Wildemere Street and spotted a corner house between Whitney and Hogarth that had a two car garage you could enter from the alley. The door on one side of the garage was missing. Bo quickly dipped in the garage and hopped out the car with her gun in hand.

After popping the trunk, she found the lone Gucci duffle bag and grabbed it without checking its contents. Bo carefully wiped her fingerprints from the door handles, gear shift and the steering wheel then grabbed her purse out the passenger seat. It took her all of ninety seconds to finish this.

Before exiting the car she looked in the backseat and saw Rochelle sitting up in her seat. "Okay, Rochelle. Thanks for being so cooperative, but this is the end of the road for you."

Rochelle's eyes looked as if they would pop out of their sockets right before Bo pulled the trigger and released two shots into her forehead. Bo was out the garage and walking down Wildemere before Rochelle's body had even slumped to the side. She didn't bother closing the trunk or the door she'd exited from.

Bo walked up Wildemere heading toward the Boulevard. On both sides of the street were huge red brick houses and a row of duplexes. Some of the houses had windows busted out of them. They all had those security bars that seemed to keep occupants trapped inside instead of keeping intruders out like they were intended to do. She paused at the red and yellow fire hydrant, sitting on the corner of Northwestern, to make sure traffic was clear before crossing the street.

"Fuck!" Bo said out loud, glancing around to make sure no one was watching her. She'd tripped over the grass that had seemed to grow over the concrete as she passed the abandoned grocery store sitting on Wildemere at Lothrop.

Bo began to get nervous when she saw two crack heads watching her from the doorway of a one story apartment complex as she approached West Grand Boulevard. Q's low key beige Toyota Camry, parked in the parking lot of an abandoned hotel that sat on the Boulevard, eased her worries.

"What the fuck you got going on, Bo?" Quincy asked as soon as she entered the car.

"Let's get out of here. Take me downtown to Chris' office," replied Bo.

Quincy pulled out the parking lot and busted a right on to West Grand Boulevard. He crossed Dexter and headed towards I96. "What the fuck is going on with you, Bo? Where is yo' car at?"

"I had to handle some unexpected business and had to leave my car parked. Now quit questioning me."

"Okay, what ever. Grab that bag out the back seat." Quincy nodded his head toward the backseat. "That's yo' money and some info on the two I need you to take care of for me."

"Cool." Bo scratched the back of her head before reaching in the backseat for the bag. *Damn! I gotta call Kim and tell her I'm still coming to get my hair and nails done. My shit itching like a muthafucka,* she thought. "You serious as hell, nigga... I could live good off your hits alone." Bo laughed.

"Niggas in the D always on some bullshit... so them niggas gotta go. This bitch ain't called the Murda Mitten for nothing. What the fuck!" Quincy said in shock as Bo began to transfer the $75,000 from the Gucci duffle bag into the bag with the $50,000 he had just given her. "I know you ain't robbed a nigga!"

"Boy, you silly as hell. I'm working, Q." Bo laughed as she placed the smaller bag with the money in it inside of the Gucci duffle bag she'd retrieved from Rochelle's trunk. She planned on burning both bags as soon as she got back home.

"Damn, I need to get a job with you then... 'cause you killin' 'em... literally and figuratively," Quincy joked.

They continued to laugh together. Quincy knew not to question Bo any further. The only time he knew someone's murder was committed by Bo was when he hired her to kill them; even then, they never spoke on it afterwards.

"So what's up for tonight?" Quincy asked. "You wanna go grab something to eat with me?"

"Are you asking me on a date, Q?" Bo joked. "You know Chris will fuck you up if he found out you was hittin' on me."

"Don't even get me started on that sorry nigga. Fuck Chris! What the fuck you see in that nigga anyway? I know you on yo' thirty second rule shit, but you know you got love for a nigga, Bo. I think Krystal would have been happy to see us together. We were the two people she loved the most. You and I will always be connected." A faraway look suddenly covered Quincy's face.

Bo sat in silence, deep in thought. She didn't say another word until Quincy pulled up to the building Chris worked in. "I already have plans for tonight, but how 'bout breakfast or lunch tomorrow?" she finally responded to Q's question.

"Just get at me, Bo," Quincy said sounding frustrated.

Bo leaned over and kissed Quincy's cheek before stepping out the car. "All right, Q. I'll talk to you later… thanks for coming to get me."

"I always got yo' back, Bonita… just remember that.

It didn't go unnoticed that Quincy had called Bo by her government name. He usually called her Bo when they were alone and only called her Bonita if others were around or if he was trying to make a point.

Bo made her way into the building and up to the floor Chris' office was on. After checking with Chris, the receptionist reluctantly escorted her to his office door. The receptionist's slight attitude was something Bo had picked up on the first time she'd ever visited Chris at his office.

She really couldn't blame her, because Chris was definitely a good catch.

Chris had graduated at the top of his class at the University of Michigan Law School and immediately accepted a position at a prestigious law firm downtown after passing the Bar Exam. He was a handsome brother with a caramel complexion, wavy hair and a very nice body. He was 6' 1" and 200 solid pounds. He had a boyish charm and a smile that could light up any room. Most importantly, in the five years Chris had been practicing law he had never lost a case.

As soon as she entered the office, Chris rushed over to embrace her. "Damn, I missed you, girl," he said while kissing her neck. "Are you hungry, sweetheart?"

"No, I still have to go back and get my hair done. I ended up leaving the shop to make a run with Q, so I just had him drop me off here. Can you take me back to my car later?"

Chris rolled his eyes up in their sockets. "What did you have to do with Q?" he inquired. "I really think he has a thing for you, Bonita. I'm uncomfortable with—"

"Look, Chris," Bo said in an aggravated tone while pulling away from Chris. "I already told you why Q and I are so close, and nothing is going to change that. If you can't deal with it… then maybe we need to stop this right now."

"No, sweetheart… I'm sorry I've upset you. It's just me being insecure. I've fallen in love with you, Bonita. Just thinking about another man with you makes me think crazy thoughts. Thoughts you could never even comprehend, sweetheart. Please forgive me."

"Chris, please don't make us have this conversation again. I came here for a reason and you're messing it up. Now lock the door and take off your clothes." Bo dropped her bag and purse on the couch and began to undress.

"What's in the bag?" Chris reached out for the Gucci duffle bag.

Bo snatched the bag before he could touch it, shocking Chris. "It's just my change of clothes for tonight... and I want it to be a surprise for you, baby."

Enough was said; Chris continued to undress and quickly made his way over to the chair sitting behind his desk. Bo was right behind him, but when she got to his desk she opted to brush everything off it and lay with her legs hanging off the edge of the desk. Chris immediately began to suck her pussy.

"Brrrrrrrrrrrr," echoed from Chris' lips as they vibrated against Bo's clit. He alternated between sticking his tongue deep up in Bo's pussy and vibrating his lips against her sensitive clit.

"Oh, shit!" Bo yelled as she enjoyed the dual sensations. She could care less she was in Chris' office and others may be able to hear her. "Yeah, Chris... just like that."

This only urged Chris to stick his tongue in even deeper, causing his nose to tickle her clit as he moved his head in an up and down motion.

Chris grabbed Bo's legs and placed them over his shoulders as he leaned over and devoured her while sitting in his chair. Her back rested on the cold cherry wood desk as she squirmed in ecstasy, occasionally opening her eyes and looking up at the florescent light fixtures on the ceiling.

After several minutes of oral pleasure, Bo finally exploded, releasing her milky mixture all over Chris' mustache, lips and beard. She quickly moved her legs from Chris' shoulders and stood up. Turning her back to Chris, she turned around and bent over the desk, displaying the sexiest ass Chris had ever hit.

"Damn, I love you, Bonita. This is my pussy," he said while sliding on the condom he'd grabbed from his top drawer. He only wore one because Bonita insisted they always use protection. Secretly, for the seven months he'd been seeing Bonita, he'd contemplated getting her pregnant just so he could always be a part of her life.

Bo waited impatiently for him to put the condom on then reached back to grab his manhood. She placed the tip of it on her pussy then popped her ass back, forcing it in. "Ohhhh," she moaned in pleasure.

"Tell me this is my pussy, Bonita. Say it's only mines, sweetheart."

As usual, Bo ignored Chris' request and continued to work her midsection, in an attempt to reach an orgasm. Even though Chris was the only person Bo was fucking at the time, she refused to give him the false hope of thinking she was only his. Bo knew in reality she was only using Chris until she left the city and was able to start her new life and hopefully settle down.

"Oh, Chris... it feels so good, baby. Fuck me harder... HARDER!!" Bo said in an attempt to bypass Chris' request.

Once again Chris was disappointed Bo would not ease his mind by telling him she was his only. Still he continued to fuck her hard—like he knew she liked it—hoping one day his wish would come true and Bo would be his and his only.

CHAPTER 3

Bo left Salon Extreme looking like a true diva. Her hair was in an updo with hanging curls framing her face. She'd gotten a manicure, pedicure, and her eyebrows and upper lip waxed. She debated getting dressed at the shop and heading downtown to meet Chris, but ended up deciding to go to her last client's house and wrap up her work for the day. She was happy to have this client's address and hoped she could catch him home alone.

As she bent the corner of Mansfield, she immediately spotted the old school Chevy just barely fitting in the driveway. Her next client Tre' and an unknown female were removing shopping bags from the trunk. "Fuck!" Bonita said, gritting her teeth. She was pissed that Tre' wasn't alone. Now she'd have to take out both of them.

Bo pulled into an empty spot in front of a house just two houses down from Tre's house and killed the lights. Even though she reloaded her gun before pulling off from the shop, she still double checked it just to make sure everything was straight. Seeing that it was, she sat back and tried to think of the best way to get this job done. Drive-by shootings were something Bo never did, because the risk of some nosey ass Good Samaritan leading the police to her was one she wasn't willing to take. Just as she was about to exit her car, she felt the vibration of her cell phone buzzing in the cup holder. It was Quincy.

"What up doe?" he asked in his typical greeting.

"What up doe?" Bo responded.

"I wanted to see if you changed yo' mind and could meet me for dinner. I really need to see you."

"Q, I told you I already have plans with Chris. What's up with breakfast tomorrow?" asked Bo.

Quincy let out a loud breath. "I need to put a hit on that nigga Chris. Hell, I'll even pay you double." He laughed.

"That shit is not funny, Q. I'm right in the middle of some work, so I'll call you when I wrap this up." Bo leaned up to tuck her gun in her waistband behind her back.

"Okay, be careful, girl. Call me when you finished."

"Okay, holla back."

Bo put her phone in her back pocket and opened the car door. She still didn't have a clue as to how she would pull this off, but this wouldn't be the first time she had to wing a hit. Each one was different and unpredictable, so it really didn't matter if she had a plan or not.

Just as she was about to step out the car, Tre' and his female companion walked toward the Chevy. After talking for a few minutes, the girl jumped in the car and slowly backed out the driveway. Tre' stood in the driveway watching her as she pulled off.

"Perfect!" Bo said with excitement in her voice. She quickly glanced at the address of the house she was parked in front of and jumped out the car, purposely slamming the car door. "Damn it!" she said loudly, faking as if she was irritated. Bo's dramatics worked as planned and got Tre's attention.

"You straight, ma?" Tre' asked. He was checking Bo out as she made her way over to the sidewalk.

"No, actually I'm lost. I was looking for 14414 Mansfield. Is that even on this block?" She continued walking towards Tre'.

"You lost as hell, baby girl." Tre' laughed. He started at her pedicured toes then worked his way up to her luscious thighs. He paused briefly at her breasts—that seemed to want to burst out of the True Religion tank top she sported. He finally made his way up to her pretty face. "I think that shit is off Schoolcraft... you on Grand River." Tre's mind raced as he tried to think of a way to holla at the beauty before Stephanie came back from the store.

"I've been driving in a circle for a while now. I can barely see the addresses now that it's getting dark out here." Bo seductively licked her bottom lip as she approached Tre'. "Do you think I could use your telephone to call my friend and ask her which way I need to go? I really don't want to keep driving around in circles. Gas is too damn high." She tried to make light of the situation.

Tre' was hesitant. He didn't trust a muthafucka and was hip to guys using a pretty female to set niggas up. He glanced to his left then to his right.

Bo sensed his hesitancy. "I'm by myself, and I really don't know this hood. It would only take me a second to call her. By the way... my name is Gloria." She extended her hand.

Tre' cautiously shook her hand, still looking up and down the street. "I'll tell you what... let me run in the crib and get my cell phone and you can use that, ma. You can't trust a muthafucka in the D."

"Thank you so much. You are really a lifesaver. Would you mind if I waited by your door while you went for the phone? I really don't know this hood... and like you said, it's scurvy as hell in the D." Bo smiled.

"That's cool." Tre' made the mistake of turning his back on Bo as they walked up to the side door. Had he been a gentleman and allowed Bo to walk in front of him, the Sig Sauer P226 would have been hard to miss.

Bo knew this was her perfect opportunity. Just as Tre' opened the side door and attempted to step inside, she quickly grabbed her weapon and forcefully stuck it in his back. "Don't be stupid, nigga," she warned him, jabbing the gun even further into his back.

"What the fuck!" Tre' yelled. He was pissed he didn't follow his first mind and tell the bitch he couldn't do nothin' for her.

"Walk yo' fat ass up them steps, nigga. And you bet not turn around, or I'ma blast yo' ass." Bo quickly locked the bottom lock on the side door as Tre walked up the three stairs leading into the kitchen.

"Just tell me what you want and get the fuck outta here." Tre' maintained his tough guy act although he was scared as hell. He knew he was in a fucked up situation and was hoping to stall her until Stephanie got back from the store. Stephanie was as hood as they came. Not only was she his lover, she was also his partner in the dope game and had saved his ass on more than one occasion. *This 'bout to be something else for this bitch to brag about,* Tre' thought. *I can hear her now... 'oh, nigga... you owe me yo' mutha fuckin' life! 'Cause you would have been dead without a bitch like me on yo' team!'*

Bo decided to save herself some time and allow Tre' to think it was just a robbery. *This really is a stupid mutha fucka if he thinks I came to rob him by myself... and at his house!* Bo thought. "You know what the fuck I want, nigga. Where the money at, mutha fucka?"

Tre' wondered how long she had been watching him and if she knew that inside two of the bags he had just carried in the house was $300,000 in drug money. "Um... I don't keep no money he—"

With no warning, Bo shot him in the right leg to let him know she wasn't bullshitting. "Don't play with me, nigga. Let's make this shit quick and easy."

Tre's eyes rolled into the back of his head as he began to feel the sting from the bullet that had silently entered his leg. "Awww shit! Bitch, you shot me!"

"And I'm aiming for the head next time. Now where the fuckin' money," Bo said through clinched teeth.

"Right here! Right here!" Tre' struggled to walk into the dining room where all the bags sat.

Bo cautiously followed him.

"Here's $150,000! Now get the fuck out!" He slid the bag toward Bo's feet.

Bo glanced down into the bag and saw it was filled with wrapped bundles of cash. "Okay, now go sit yo' ass on the floor in the corner over there." She used the gun to point in the direction she was speaking of.

Tre' quickly complied. He just wanted the crazy bitch to get the fuck out. Losing $150,000 was nothing to him. He knew he could make that back the next day. *I'ma kill this fuckin' bitch when I find her ass,* he thought.

Once Tre' was in the corner Bo looked down into the other bags. She immediately spotted a second bag filled with cash. "Ohhhhh… so you holdin' out on me, Tre'," she said with a wide grin on her face.

A look of shock spread across Tre's face once she said his name. This let him know this was no random act and someone had really set him up. His shocked look didn't go unnoticed by Bo.

"Okay, Tre'. Do you want to know who put the hit on you?" Bo asked in her customary manner.

"The hit! What the fuck you talkin' 'bout… hit?" Sweat began to pour down Tre's face. His heart rate increased, and his palms began to sweat. His eyes were bulging out so far they were starting to make his head hurt.

"You shouldn't have robbed that nigga Pooh, Tre'," Bo said in a sing song voice. "Did you think he was gon' let you get on after taking his money and do nothing about it? Come on now… I know you ain't that stupid."

"That hoe ass nigga Pooh set me up? I knew I shoulda killed that nigga when I robbed his hoe ass." Tre' couldn't believe that after eight months the nigga Pooh he had jacked for $100,000 was trying to get some get back.

"Yep." Bo fired one shot that entered Tre's left eye before continuing. "You should have killed 'em." She walked up on him and fired a second shot that hit him in the forehead.

Quickly grabbing both bags of money, Bo made her way toward the side door. Just as she approached the kitchen she heard keys jiggling in the door. Stepping to the side and out of view from the entryway, she sat the bags down and positioned her gun to fire.

"Baby! Baby!" Stephanie yelled as she swung the door open. "I know you hear me, nigga! I stopped and got a pizza so you—" she stopped mid-sentence after seeing Tre's legs sprawled out across the floor. She could only see his legs due to the angles of the entryways. "Tre'!" she screamed at the top of her lungs as she dropped the pizza and the bag she was carrying.

Stephanie quickly pulled her .22 from her purse as she ran up the stairs. As she was running through the kitchen she spotted the glare from the shiny chrome of Bo's gun and let off a wild shot toward Bo. She ran through the kitchen and dining room toward the stairs leading to the master bedroom.

Bo fired two shots as she dived to the left, bumping her head on the cabinets below the kitchen sink. "I'ma kill this stupid bitch!" she said out loud, rubbing her head with her free hand. She could tell the girl was running up stairs. On second thought, Bo decided to make a break, hoping the girl didn't have time to see her face clearly. She didn't know what kind of weapons they kept in the house and wasn't trying to find out.

This would prove to be a wise choice for Bo, because Stephanie had grabbed the AK47 Tre' kept in the corner closest to the bed. She was in a blind rage as she ran back down the stairs and headed toward the kitchen. Just as she reached the side door she cocked the AK. She had figured the bitch would bail, so she headed straight out the door and ran down the driveway.

Bo had run full speed to her car and jumped in, throwing the two bags in the passenger seat and putting the key in the ignition at the same time. As she pulled away from the curb, she could see the girl running down the driveway with an AK. "Fuck!" she yelled as she put the gas pedal to the floor, burning rubber as she took off. She could only say a silent prayer as she sped off, heading right into the path of the AK's deadly wrath.

BOOM! BOOM! BOOM! BOOM! BOOM!

The first missile shaped bullet ripped through the back passenger side door of Bo's Benz penetrating the metal and exiting the driver's side door. The others grazed the trunk of the Benz. Miraculously, Bo escaped unscathed, whipping the corner at 80 mph, damn near on two wheels.

Bo blew past the stop sign at St. Marys Street and rode down Lyndon until she came upon the Southfield Service Drive. She tried to blend in with traffic as she crossed the lights at Grand River and Fenkell then merged onto the Southfield Freeway going north. There was no way she was going to the crib. Still visibly upset and looking out for the Chevy, Bo grabbed her cell phone and hit number one on the speed dial. Her hands were shaking as she gripped the steering wheel with one hand while holding the phone with the other.

"What up doe, baby?" Quincy answered on the first ring.

"I just almost got my fuckin' head blew off. That's what the fuck is up!"

"What! What the fuck happened? Where you at? I'm on my way!" Quincy spit out rapidly.

"I'm on Southfield crossing Seven Mile! You at home?" Bo was going 110 mph, weaving in and out of traffic.

"Yeah... what the fuck happened?" Quincy paced the floor of the living room in his ranch style home. He took a long pull from the blunt hanging from his mouth.

"I'm headed yo' way. I'll tell you about it when I get there. Open the garage so I can pull in," said Bo before pressing the end button on the phone.

Bo began to calm down a little once she reached the point where the Southfield Freeway ran out. She made a left turn at Ten Mile and headed west to Barbara Fritchie Street. Going right on Barbara Fritchie she drove down to Hilton Street where she made another right and drove a few houses down until she got to Quincy's house. She whipped up in the long driveway and sped into the opened two car garage.

Quincy was standing at the side door with an AR-15 in one hand and a lit blunt in the other. He stuck his head out the door to glance down the street, making sure there was no one following Bo. Feeling safe the coast was clear, he rushed out to the garage to make sure she was all right.

Bo jumped out the car and headed toward Quincy. "Close the garage, Q. Let's go in the house," she said with panic in her voice.

Once they made it inside, Quincy closed the garage and led Bo into the living room. "Now what the fuck just happened?"

Bo grabbed the blunt from Q's mouth and took a deep pull. She rarely smoke weed, but needed something to calm her nerves.

Quincy walked over to the bar and poured a glass of Remy Martin for Bo. He knew she needed it, because he had never seen her look so shook, and she was killing the blunt even though she didn't really smoke. "Here, sip this," he said, passing her the glass.

The hot brown liquid saturated Bo's tongue before going down her throat surprisingly smooth. Once the glass was empty, she held it out for Quincy to refill. After downing her second drink and taking another pull from the blunt, she sat down on the coach and began to tell Q what had just happened to her.

CHAPTER 4

Bo pulled the Camry in her garage and headed to the trunk. After grabbing her purse, the backpack she took from Rahiem at the hotel that morning, the Gucci duffle bag she got from Rochelle's trunk and the two bags she'd taken from Tre', she struggled to carry them all through the garage and to the door that led into her kitchen. She had left her car parked in Quincy's garage and taken the rental he'd picked her up in earlier that day.

Making sure to secure the door, she headed upstairs to her bedroom and dumped all the cash she'd made that day on her bed. She didn't count it out, but there was $425,000 counting the $50,000 Quincy had paid her for the dope and the three hits he ordered. This was the most she had ever scored in one day's work.

"I guess that fat mutha fucka Tre' was worth all the trouble after all," she joked, stuffing the cash back inside the bag and tossing it to the side. "Damn!" she cursed herself. She had left the outfit she planned on wearing tonight in her trunk during the rush to get the cash in the Camry's trunk.

After settling on a sexy black lace panty and bra set to wear under a little black Chanel dress, she searched her shoe racks for her black Manolo stilettos then grabbed a small Chanel purse. Once she'd laid her new outfit for the night out on the bed, she filled the tub with mostly hot water and Calgon Ocean Breeze. After a long days work a hot Calgon bath was just what Bo needed to unwind before heading downtown to meet Chris.

Once the tub was filled to the rim, Bo slid out of her clothes and slowly eased one foot in the hot bath. Feeling the scalding hot water, she jerked her foot back then added more cold water until the temperature was just right. Slowly lowering herself in the hot water, she lay her head back onto the pink bath pillow and closed her eyes.

BAM! BAM! BAM! BAM! BAM!

Bo jolted awake at the sound of the loud banging at her door. Jumping from the tub, she quickly grabbed her pink terrycloth bath wrap and secured the Velcro fastener. Not many people knew where she rested her head, and out of the few who did know none would have the balls to show up at her place unannounced. Bo grabbed the Desert Eagle she kept in the cabinet under the bathroom sink and headed for the door.

After carefully looking out the peephole, she opened the door to find Quincy standing there with the bag that contained the outfit she'd forgotten to retrieve from her car earlier. He was now wearing a pair of casual slacks and a short sleeved button up shirt with matching gators. Unable to totally let go of the hood in him, he donned a traditional blue and white Detroit Tigers baseball hat.

"What the hell you doing here… and why didn't you call first?" Bo asked without offering Quincy the opportunity to come inside.

Quincy's eyes slowly traveled the length of Bo's body in the short bath wrap. "Girl, let me in this mutha fucka. I came to do you a favor," he replied, sticking the bag in her face and pushing his way into the house.

"You could have called! Damn! Interrupting my bath and shit," Bo complained, although she was happy he had woken her up. "I already picked out something else to wear tonight anyway." She secured the locks on the door and turned away to go into her bedroom.

Quincy watched her ass jiggle as he followed behind her, subconsciously adjusting his rapidly growing dick. "See, I ain't never doing shit else for yo' unappreciative ass. I'm on my way downtown to pop some bottles... get dressed and you can roll with me."

"Q, I told you I'm meeting Chris downtown tonight for drinks. You just don't take no for an answer, huh?"

Quincy placed the bag on the floor once they had reached Bo's room then quickly grabbed her up in an embrace. "That nigga Chris can't make you feel like I can," he said before thrusting his tongue in her mouth.

At first he felt Bo's resistance, but moments later she'd began to reciprocate the passionate kiss. This gave Quincy the courage needed to roughly grip Bo's ass, feeling its softness through the terrycloth.

What the hell am I doing? Bo thought as she felt herself getting moist while tonguing down Q. The feel of his hands gripping her ass was turning her on like she had never been turned on before—except that one time, of course. Her moisture built and soon began to drip from her pussy like a faucet, leaving small drops on the floor space directly between her legs.

Continuing to kiss her, Quincy spun Bo around until her back was to the bed, pushed her down on it and lay on top of her, never breaking their kiss. She opened her eyes and was now staring directly into his.

"Shhhhhh," Quincy said, placing his index finger over her lips to hush her. Bo pulled her lips away from his and was attempting to say something.

Q released the Velcro's grip and stared down at Bo's body. He had never seen a body as perfect as hers, which instantly made his dick as hard as a cement block. Lowering his head to her chest, he began to circle her right nipple with his tongue.

"Ummmm," Bo moaned. "Q, wait." She wiggled in an attempt to get out of his grip, but he had her arms lifted above her head and the weight of his body kept her in place. "Q... we... we can't do this," she continued to protest.

"I love you, Bo. I'm in love with you," Quincy said between licks. "This shit is just right. We need to be together." Quincy released her hands and stuck his right, middle finger deep into her pussy. Removing it, he lifted his head from her breast and inserted the wet finger in his mouth, savoring every bit of her juices. "Let me make love to you, Bo. Please." He placed his finger back inside her and made a slow circular motion.

"This ain't right, Q," Bo continued to protest, although she didn't stop him or attempt to get up.

The feeling he was providing her with felt much too good for her to stop him. She knew she was just moments away from breaking her thirty second rule, because if sex with Q was going to make her feel better than she felt at that moment there was no way she would be able to walk out of his life afterwards. She allowed him to continue to pleasure her and soon they were kissing once again.

Quincy couldn't believe after years of yearning for Bo he was finally about to fuck her. He planned on blowing her back out so good she would be sprung and begging for more on a daily basis. He broke their kiss and made a trial of kisses down the center of her chest and down to her stomach before finally reaching her heart shaped patch of pubic hairs. He licked the heart, causing Bo to shutter then continued downward until he was able to cover her outer lips with the ones on his face. He locked his arms around her thighs and pulled her legs apart as far as they would go. Next, he proceeded to tongue her pussy by sticking his tongue deep inside and attempting to lick all of its walls.

The feel of Q's lips around her pussy was driving Bo crazy, but once he stuck his tongue deep inside her, she was in pure ecstasy. This was the first time she had been eaten out so expertly, and the feel of his mouth covering her entire pussy was indescribable. His goatee was tickling the space between her pussy and her asshole as he tongued her. In the back of her mind she was telling herself they needed to stop, but the pleasure he was giving her would not allow her to do so.

"Whhhy, Q? Why... you doing this to me?" Bo moaned in bliss. "I... ssssss... I... ssssss... I can't take it, Q. I'm... about... to... to cum," Bo said, before cumming inside Q's mouth.

Satisfied with his performance, Q lifted his head to look at Bo, who was laid back with her eyes closed and panting loudly. He had creamy goo covering his lips from when he kissed Bo's pussy after making her shoot off in his mouth. He went back down to lick any remaining cum from Bo's pussy before kissing it then jumping up and beginning to remove his clothes.

"Wait, Q," Bo said once she'd caught her breath and looked up to see him undressing. "I really can't do this. You're like a brother to me."

"WHAT! I wasn't like yo' brother when I had you moaning and groaning a minute ago." Quincy had removed his shirt and let it fall to the floor. He proceeded to pull his pants and boxers down in one motion, allowing nine and a half inches of hard dick to spring up way past his navel. "Why you fighting this shit, Bo? You know we would be good together."

Bo jumped up at the sight of Q's huge dick. It was a chocolate brown complexion and the most beautiful one she had ever seen. She pulled her bath wrap back around her body, securing the Velcro and quickly sat up, placing her at eye level with Q's pretty dick.

"We probably would be good together, Q. I can't even deny the fact that I'm attracted to you, but this just don't feel right."

"Did it feel right when you bust a nut in my mouth?" Quincy asked sarcastically.

"I know... I should have stopped you before it got that far. I'm sorry, Q." Bo stood up and attempted to go back to the bathroom but was stopped when Quincy grabbed her by the forearm.

"So you just gon' leave me like this?" Quincy nodded down toward his erect penis. "I know you not gon' leave me like this, Bo," he reiterated.

"I said I'm sorry. What you want me to do?" Bo snatched her arm away and continued toward the bathroom.

"Shit! You can give me some pussy, suck it, give me a hand job... do something, girl!" Quincy yelled out.

"Wait a minute," Bo responded. She grabbed a clean towel from the linen closet and a bottle of Vaseline Intensive Care with Aloe Vera lotion from the medicine cabinet before heading back to her bedroom.

Quincy was still standing in the same spot with his dick pointing toward the ceiling. He had a puzzled look on his face when he saw the items Bo was carrying. "So what's up?" he asked.

"Here," Bo said, passing him the towel and lotion. "You can use the downstairs bathroom," she said in a matter of fact manner.

"Use the downstairs bathroom? And do what?" questioned Quincy.

"Get yo' self off, nigga. You know what's up," Bo responded before turning on her heels and heading back to the bathroom to shower.

Quincy stood there dumbfounded before finally grabbing his clothes from the floor and heading for the downstairs bathroom. "This is some bullshit!" he mumbled to himself. "If I didn't really care about this bitch I'd take the fuckin' pussy," he continued to complain.

As Bonita showered upstairs, Quincy envisioned her fat pussy with the heart-shaped patch of hair as he rubbed the lotion in his hands and began to slow stroke his piece. It wasn't hard to get into it after the episode that had just occurred upstairs. Minutes later, cum shot from his dick into his hand. A few drops shot up, speckling the bathroom mirror.

Quincy wet and lathered a corner of the towel and washed his private parts. After rinsing all the soap off, he dried the area and put his clothes back on. "That's all right, she gon' clean that shit off her mirror since she playing wit' a nigga and shit," he said to himself, exiting the bathroom.

Bo was already dressed and putting on her jewelry when Quincy came back in her room. She could feel his eyes on her ass as she stood in front of the mirror. As hard as she was trying, she could not get the thought of how good he had just made her feel out her mind.

Quincy threw the dirty towel and lotion bottle on Bo's bed then walked up behind her. He made sure he was close enough to graze his dick against her ass. "I'm out of here. You can take my Hummer... I'm trying to be low key tonight. I'll drive the rental," he said, gazing at her through the mirror.

"Okay, let me get the keys for you." Bo moved from in front of Quincy and made her way over to the nightstand. "Ughh! Nigga, why the fuck you put that nasty shit on my bed?" She grabbed the partially wet towel and lotion from her bed and threw it to the floor. "You could have took that shit with you... with yo' trifling ass!"

Quincy laughed at her. "If you would have handled yo' business then I wouldn't have needed that shit. I would have cum all up inside that fat pussy." He playfully hit Bo on the ass.

"I don't know what the fuck done got into you, Q, but you tripping. Please don't let this shit fuck up our friendship," she said seriously, looking him in the eyes.

Quincy grabbed the keys to the rental from her and threw the spare keys to the Hummer on her nightstand. "Bo, I ain't even trippin' on that shit. As tasty as yo' shit is... I'll come eat it whenever you want me to, and we still gon' be fam."

"Shut up, boy! I'm serious, Q. I don't want this shit to make us act funny around each other. We was meant to be fam... and that's it." Bo returned to the mirror and began to apply her make-up.

"We'll see, Bo." Quincy glanced at her ass again before heading for the door.

"Wait! Let me get the door, nigga... oh, you in a rush now?" Bo followed him to the side door.

"Naw, but if I stay here any longer I might just have to take that shit from you. Oh, and the spare house key is on there with the Hummer key, so if you don't wanna go home when you leave the club you can come to my crib," Quincy joked but was dead serious.

"Bye, boy! Hey, where the truck at?" Bo said as she pressed the button to open the garage.

"It's in front of the house. I figured you had the Camry in the garage." Quincy looked back at Bo and said, "Be safe out here tonight."

"You, too... I'll call you tomorrow."

After closing and locking the side door, Bo went back upstairs and put on her shoes then put the necessary items from her Gucci bag into the Chanel purse she was carrying. She grabbed a stack of cash from the bag on the floor, placed it in her purse then secured the bag in her floor safe in the closet before heading downstairs to leave the house.

Bo was happy to see Q had the Hummer shinned up. The black and chrome truck matched her outfit and jewelry perfectly. After a long day putting in work she planned on letting herself get a little loose with Chris at the club tonight. After starting up the truck she was pleased to hear Jay-Z's *Reasonable Doubt* in the CD player. One of her favorite songs, "Can't Knock the Hustle" was banging from the system.

After bending a few corners, Bo was cruising down Seven Mile headed east to the Lodge Freeway. She'd just crossed Greenfield when she noticed the flashing lights behind the truck. "Fuck!" she said out loud, her nerves quickly getting the best of her.

She was hoping Q wasn't dumb enough to have any drugs in the truck, but that wasn't her only fear. She knew he kept a compact Glock 19 in the glove compartment at all times. She also knew the fact that she didn't think to get the registration or proof of insurance may cause the police to fuck with her. After pulling her drivers license out her purse, she lowered the window and stuck it out to the officer—who's eyes were scouring the inside of the truck.

"Good evening, Miss. Is this your vehicle?" he asked, taking the license from her hand and looking at it.

"No, this is my cousin's truck. I'm just borrowing it for the night," Bo replied.

"Where you headed," the officer continued to question.

"I'm meeting my friend downtown for a drink." Bo noticed how the officer's eyes were all over the inside of the truck. By this time, his partner had also stepped out the police car and was flashing his flashlight inside the truck from the passenger's side.

The second officer tapped on the window with his flashlight, indicating he wanted Bo to lower the window. Once it was lowered he asked, "You been smoking in here?"

"No, Sir. I don't smoke," she lied. She knew they were fucking with her, because she didn't smell any weed in the truck. In fact, it smelled like it had just been detailed and had a watermelon air freshener hanging from the gear shift.

The officer with her license walked back to the police car while the second officer continued to interrogate Bo. "So, where are you off to in such a rush?" he asked, licking his lips seductively.

Bo did everything she could to keep her composure. She knew they were just fucking with her because they probably couldn't see her through the tints and thought she was a nigga. "I'm going to a club downtown to meet up with my friend," she repeated.

"What about after that?" he caught her off guard by asking.

Bo took a closer look at the officer before answering. He was about 5' 10" with a muscular build. He was a light complexion and had a sexy mustache. She couldn't see his hair because he was wearing his hat. "Excuse me?" she replied.

"You think I could take you out for coffee or maybe breakfast after you meet your friend?" he bluntly asked.

Bo exhaled a sigh of relief. At this point she knew she could talk her way out of this situation. "I don't know," she toyed with him. "Can I step out the truck and come over there so I can get a good look at you," she flirted.

"Sure, step out the truck," he told her as the first officer made his way back over.

Bo slowly opened the door and stuck her leg out the truck. She looked up to see the approaching officer staring at her as she jumped out the Hummer.

"I asked her to step out the truck," the flirting officer explained to his partner, who looked dumb struck after getting a full view of Bo in her short dress and stilettos.

Bo noticed he didn't have a ticket in his hand, so she felt even more comfortable as she switched over to the sidewalk where the officer stood. His partner followed her over as well.

"Damn you looking good!" the flirty officer responded after getting a full view of Bo.

"Thank you, you're not so bad yourself," she flirted back.

The officers joked back and forth about who should get Bo's number then both ended up giving her their business card and said they'd wait to see who she called later on that morning when she left the club. Bo thanked them for giving her a warning for going five miles over the speed limit and got back inside the truck.

As soon as she made it to the Lodge Freeway she threw both business cards out the window and turned up "Friend or Foe." Bo looked in the glove compartment to make sure the Glock was in there and was happy to see it was. Had it not been, she was planning on turning back around to go home for some heat.

CHAPTER 5

The club was packed as hell just as Bo expected it to be. She pulled the Hummer behind a black Bentley Coup and waited for Valet to make their way to her. Once she received her valet ticket, she made her way inside and bumped right into Quincy.

"What the hell are you doing here? You stalking me or what?" she joked. "And why the fuck you got that Glock in the glove compartment? I just got flicked by the Detroit Police and could have been doing a mandatory two years behind that bullshit."

"You know I keep that gun in the Hummer. And if it wasn't there you would have had one on you anyway. I know how you roll, Bo." Quincy grabbed her hand and led her over to the bar. "Come on… let me buy you a bottle," he insisted.

As they made their way to the bar several guys looked at Quincy with envy in their eyes. A few guys even stopped him to give him dap and let him know he was with the baddest bitch in the club. Once they reached the bar, a stank looking bartender approached them and openly flirted with Quincy.

"Hey, Q… you know I got you all night, baby. What you need?" She had on tight blue jeans with rips all over them, exposing her ass cheeks. Her red halter top left nothing to the imagination. Her hair was also red—one of those quick weaves.

"What up doe, Sonya?" Quincy responded. "Let me get a triple shot of Remy on the rocks and get my girl a bottle of black label Moët."

"Oh, that's yo' girl, Q?" she inquired.

Bo stepped up to the bar. "Bitch, just get the damn drinks and stop worrying about who the fuck I am. And don't open my shit either." Bo's outburst shocked both Quincy and Sonya.

"What's wrong with yo' girl, Q. I was just asking—"

"Sonya, just get the drinks. I'll holla at you later," Quincy cut her off.

Sonya proceeded to grab the Remy bottle and poured Quincy's drink then reached in the cooler to get the bottle of champagne. "How many glasses," she asked looking at Quincy.

"One," Bo answered.

Once they had their drinks, Quincy led Bo over to a table in the back of the club where two of his boys were sitting. The table was already full of bottles of Dom Pérignon and Moët as well as two fifths of Remy.

"Why you get these drinks if you already had all this shit over here," Bo asked while Q opened her bottle and poured her a glass.

"Cause I saw you coming in and had to divert you from going straight over to that lame ass nigga Chris. I'm surprised his ass is even up in here." Q and his boys laughed. "Plus, we about to get fucked up!" he said, all hyped up.

The DJ was playing Young Jeezy's song "Gangsta Music." The two guys at Q's table stood up with bottles in their hands and Errol Flynned like it was the 80's. Bo downed her first glass of Moët and poured herself another.

"So where did you see Chris at?" she asked Q, yelling over the loud music.

"Fuck Chris," was Q's response. "Why don't you leave here with me, so we can finish what we started at yo' place?"

Just as Bo was about to respond, she noticed a visibly upset Chris making his way over to Q's table. "Let me go talk to him," she said, trying to squeeze her way past Quincy, who had blocked her in.

"Fuck that nigga," Q said loud enough for Chris to hear. "He gon' fuck around and get fucked up tonight."

"Fa-fa-fa-fa sho," Q's stuttering boy Jay shouted.

Chris approached the table like he didn't have a fear in the world. Although he knew Quincy and the crowd he hung out with would make good on their promises, he refused to let them punk him in front of Bonita. "Hey, sweetheart... our table is across the room," he said to Bonita.

"I'm coming now, Chris. I just stopped over here to have a drink with Q." Bo squeezed past Q and grabbed Chris' outreached hand.

"Don't forget to take yo' bottle," Quincy said, attempting to hand Bo the bottle.

"No need for that," Chris interjected. "I know what *my* girl likes, and I have a couple of bottles and some fresh strawberries at our table for her. Thanks for taking care of her until I got over here," he said sarcastically.

Quincy stood up with the bottle still in his hand. His boys stopped partying and were ready to follow Q's lead.

"It's cool, Q. I'll bring your truck back to you in the morning." Bo released Chris' hand and turn around to give Q a hug before walking off with Chris.

"I wanna fuck that hoe ass nigga up so bad!" Quincy vented once they were gone.

"Yo-yo-yo-yo-yo-yo-you sh-sh-sh-sh-sh-should of fu-fu-fu-fucked th-th—"

"All, nigga shut the fuck up!" Q's other boy Arnell said. "We a be all night tryna get one sentence outta yo' stuttering ass!"

They all laughed and got back into party mode.

On the other side of the club Bonita sat at a table with Chris and three other lawyers from his office. As promised, there were bottles of Moët and fresh strawberries on the table. Chris poured Bonita a glass of Moët and put a strawberry in it.

"Thanks," Bo said, accepting the glass from him.

"No problem, sweetheart. I told you I got you," Chris said trying to sound cool.

About an hour passed and Bonita was bored out of her mind. The discussion had been centered on the various cases the lawyers were currently working on. No one had even attempted to include Bonita in the conversation. She found herself wondering what Q was doing over at his table.

"I'll be back, Chris. I'm going to the restroom," she said as soon as she could get a word in edge wise.

"I'll walk you over there, sweetheart," Chris offered.

"No!" Bo said a little too abruptly. "I know there is going to be a long line, and I don't want to keep you away from your friends for too long. I want to leave in a few minutes anyway. It's getting way too crowded up in here for me," she lied and quickly walked away from the table.

Bo hadn't taken ten steps before the first guy approached her. "Hey, sexy," he said, grabbing her wrist. "Can I get you a bottle or something?"

He was an all right looking guy; dark-skinned, dressed nice and wearing at least $50,000 worth of jewelry, but he was only about 5' 4" and clearly weighed over 200 pounds. His stomach stuck out like a women ready to deliver at any moment.

Bo gently released her wrist before replying, "I'm fine, I'm with my boyfriend."

"Damn, baby. You look too good for me to just let you pass. Can I at least give you my number and you can call me later?" he persisted.

"Fat Man, I know you not trying to holla at my girl?" a familiar voice yelled out.

Bo turned around to once again find Q coming toward her.

"Awww, man, Q you always got a fine ass girl wit' you, nigga," Fat Man said, trying to piss Bo off.

"You damn right, nigga... and this one mines, too," Q responded, not missing Fat Man's slick remark.

Quincy grabbed Bo's hand and led her down the hallway leading to the restrooms. Once they reached the line for the ladies room, he stopped to wait with her. "Leave with me now," he whispered in her ear. "Come on, Bo."

A part of her wanted to do just that. She was still having flashbacks of their episode earlier in the day. "Q, quit playing so much. You know I'm here with Chris," she reminded him.

"You know that nigga can't fuck you like I can. Don't you?" he persisted.

Bo rushed in the restroom to avoid having to answer his question. Once inside, she still had to wait for a stall to become available before she could go in and pee. A few minutes later, a light-skinned, short, fat girl with pimples all over her face came out a stall and walked over to the sink.

Bo made her way in the stall and pulled her panties down. She squatted over the nasty toilet seat and proceeded to piss for at least a minute. As she pissed, she looked at all the toilet paper scattered across the floor. There was even a bloody maxi pad hanging out the chrome box that was meant for them to be placed inside of. Bo exhaled as her pee finally came to an end. She quickly wiped herself and exited the stall.

"It's nasty as hell in there," Bo said to the girl waiting to enter the stall after her.

"It always is," the girl smiled and replied.

After washing her hands and freshening up her make-up, Bo made her way out the bathroom. Q was still standing there waiting on her.

"About time," he complained. "So we leaving now?" he asked.

"What did I just tell you, Q? I'm—" Bo stopped talking mid-sentence as she spotted the girl who was shooting at her at her last hit. The girl had spotted and recognized Bo as well.

Stephanie couldn't believe the bitch that had killed Tre' just hours ago was partying like a rock star at the club. She was about to approach her, but thought against it when she saw her with Q, who was well known in the city. Instead, she made her way to the door so she could get her gun out the car. After the incident at Tre's house, Stephanie had run back inside the house to grab the money before fleeing the scene. She was pissed off when she noticed both bags were gone and quickly left empty handed.

Once Bo saw Stephanie heading for the door she knew what was up. "Is there a back way out this club?" she asked Q. "I need to get out of here ASAP. I just saw the bitch that was at the house I made my last hit at."

"What! You fuckin' wit' me, right?" asked Quincy.

"Hell naw I'm not fucking with you, Q! I parked yo' truck with the Valet and this bitch just headed toward the front door! This is the same bitch that just fucked my car up with an AK!"

"Come on." Q grabbed her hand and began to lead her toward the emergency exit. He'd parked his car a block away from the club because he hated to have to wait for Valet after the club let out. Many niggas got killed waiting on Valet to get their cars once the club had closed.

"Bonita! What's going on?" Chris asked as he saw her and Q rushing toward the emergency exit. "Why are you with him again? You're supposed to be here with me."

Bonita ignored Chris, quickly implementing her thirty second rule. Just as Q reached for the door, it was forced opened and the Detroit Police swarmed the club. Bo looked toward the front door and noticed police were entering the club from that entrance as well. Unsure of what to do next, Bo and Q stood frozen in place.

It couldn't have been a worse time for Chris to grow some balls, but he finally did. He grabbed Bonita's hand and attempted to shield her from the growing commotion inside the club. Bonita stood just inches away from the exit with police all around her. Quincy held one of her hands and Chris held the other.

What the fuck have I gotten myself into now? I wish I would have just stayed home and let Q fuck the shit out of me. This is some straight up bullshit, Bo thought as the police attempted to restore order in the club.

Both exits were blocked and Bonita had nowhere to run. She didn't have a clue what or who the police were after. But one thing was for sure; she knew Stephanie was waiting for her to exit the club.

CHAPTER 6

"Bonita. If you don't come with me right now I'm through with you. I'm not going to continue to allow this street thug to come before me. Now who are you going to leave with," Chris demanded.

Just as Bo snatched away from both Q and Chris, a fierce punch from Quincy landed square into Chris' jaw. At four inches taller and sixty-five pounds heavier, Q's one punch made Chris buckle. This caused a gang of officers to come over and intervened; taking both Chris and Q directly outside the club and getting rid of Bo's problem for the moment.

Loud chatter could be heard throughout the club as the music abruptly stopped. The police quickly established order in the club, separating the patrons by the people who valet parked and those who didn't. Bo noticed a shady looking guy walking up to get in line behind her. She glanced at him from head to toe, noticing a bruise on his eye and a lump on his nose.

"This is some bullshit," Bo mumbled out loud without realizing it.

"Hell mutha fuckin' yeah!" the guy responded.

Bo glanced outside the large windows showing the view of the front of the club. There were people and police fluttering about outside the club.

"I wonder what the fuck this is about." Bo said to no one in particular. She was anxious to get to the Hummer and get the hell out of there. She still didn't know what was going on. The police were going down the lines checking IDs before allowing people to leave the club. "How long we gon' be in this bitch!" she yelled out to a passing officer.

"Damn, ma... slow ya roll," the stranger spoke again.

"Why you people can't follow instructions?" the white cop replied as he continued to walk to the front of the line.

Bo turned to the guy and said, "Did you hear that shit?"

"Yeah, ma... but don't let that shit bother you."

"I had a fucked up day. I'm just ready to get the fuck out of here." Bo nervously shifted from foot to foot.

"I feel you... my day been pretty fucked up, too."

Bo watched as the weirdo stared out the window.

"Oh, hell naw," he mumbled. He walked over to the trash can and tossed his valet ticket then stepped back in line.

Bo noticed one of the officers who had pulled her over earlier and waved to get his attention. She was determined to get out of there by any means necessary. The officer instantly remembered Bo and rushed over to talk to her.

"Hey, I was just about to call you to hook up when this shit happened," she said smiling at him.

The officer, oblivious to everything but the fact that Bo was choosing him, replied, "So I guess you chose me then, Bonita." He smiled broadly.

"You thought I wouldn't?" Bo said seductively. She noticed the shady looking stranger peeping her game. "Hey... can you get me out of here? That would give me time to go home and freshen up before hooking up with you once you finish up here."

"Hell yeah! Come on," he said, grabbing her arm and heading toward the front door.

The must be psychotic stranger grabbed Bo's other arm. "Hold up! I know you ain't gon' leave me hangin'?"

Bo could see the desperation in his eyes and sympathized with him. Judging by the looks of him, including the chipped tooth she noticed once he'd started talking, he was in a bad situation.

"Hey, can my cousin get out of here, too? We met down here and I'm his ride," Bo asked. The officer looked him over before waving for him to come on as well.

"Damn, good lookin', Bonita."

"You straight." Bo responded, pausing for him to tell her his name as they flowed to the front of the line.

"Tusconi," he replied.

Once they got to the door the officer told the other officer at the door they were checked out and cleared. He got Bo's keys from the officer and handed them to her.

"I betta hear from you tonight," the officer said to Bo.

"Oh, you will, sweetie." Relieved she was finally getting out the club, Bo quickly walked away.

"I know this shit is beyond the call of duty, but can you give a nigga a ride?"

Bo frowned up and looked at Tusconi like he'd lost his mind. She followed his eyes over to a BMW parked in front of the club. Sitting on the hood of the car were a couple of low budget bitches talking to none other than Stephanie.

"I guess," Bo replied. "Damn, where to?"

"Eastside... or how about the MGM?"

"That's cool."

Bo glanced over at the weird looking character she had just agreed to drop off at the MGM Casino. Usually she would have never allowed a stranger to ride with her, but he looked like his day had been even more fucked up than hers.

Police were out in full force and urged everyone to leave the premises immediately. Bo and the stranger walked at a brisk pace as they headed toward the Hummer. Bo followed the stranger's eyes as he again looked at the BMW they were approaching.

"See you later," Bo said to Stephanie with a smirk on her face as they walked past.

"Keep it moving," an officer approached Stephanie and her girls and said to them.

Stephanie grimed Bo until she was out of sight. She was pissed off at herself for locking her keys in the car in her hurry to get inside the club to meet her girls. Although she was in no partying mood, her girls had convinced her to come out for a drink in memory of Tre'. After sitting in her apartment going out of her mind with thoughts of Tre', she finally decided to get out the house and ended up at the club. Now she was forced to sit and watch the bitch that killed Tre' and took all the money they'd just picked up make a smooth get-a-way. *Tre', I swear to God I'm gon' kill that bitch, baby. I promise you that,* Stephanie thought.

Bo hopped in the Hummer and immediately grabbed the Glock from the glove compartment. "No offense, but I don't know you," she said to the stranger.

"Damn, Bonita. You straight gangsta. You can get to know me," Tusconi said as he tugged on the crouch of his pants.

"Look... don't make me change my mind about the ride. And quit calling me Bonita. To you... my name is Bo!" Bo was getting irritated with Tusconi and thought about putting his ass out... literally.

"Yeah, alright. Damn! Excuse the fuck out of me. You's one of them high class broads."

Bo overlooked his smart comment and stepped on the gas in an attempt to get to the MGM as soon as possible.

Tusconi peered through the rearview mirror until the club was no longer in sight. The truck was silent for the short ride to the MGM.

Pulling up at the MGM moments later, Bo glanced over at Tusconi.

"Be safe," Bo said as Tusconi opened the door to exit the truck.

"You sure I can't go with you?"

"Boy, bye!" Bo laughed in his face and skirted off, causing the door to shut itself.

Bo decided to head over to Q's place. She grabbed her phone from her purse and pressed number one to speed dial him. Q answered on the first ring.

"What up doe? Where you at?" he questioned.

"I'm on my way to your house. Where are you?"

"When they separated me from Chris they checked me out and let me leave the club. I'm at home now. Come on... we 'bout to get a spades game going."

Bo could hear others in the background laughing and joking around. "Damn! You having a party over there? I might as well go to the crib. I'm just trying to chill out after all the shit that went down today, Q."

"Girl, bring ya' ass. These my peeps from Vegas... and my cousin Rio."

"Like I fuck with them niggas, Q. I'm bringing you yo' truck and you can take me to the crib. I ain't trying to play spades. Bye." Bo hung up before he could respond. While she really didn't want to go home alone, she wasn't trying to be around a bunch of people either. And she especially wasn't trying to see Rio. Bo thought back to a time when life was much simpler for her.

Krystal and Bonita had been inseparable since third grade. They lived just a few blocks away from each other but would usually play at Bonita's house since she lived closest to the school and had all the latest Barbie's with matching accessories. The girls initially met the first day of class when a crew of girls decided they didn't like Bonita, with her new clothes and long ponytails. The girls were all much bigger than Bonita, who was small for her age. Once the kids were let outside for recess, the girls began to circle poor Bonita, who was frightened to death.

"You think you so cute," the leader of the pack said, yanking Bonita's ponytail roughly. "You ain't cute little white girl!"

Bonita frantically searched for a way out of the situation. Bonita was an only child and had never been in a fist fight in her life. Her parents had kept her sheltered from the harsh realities of life, providing her with all the material things she could ever desire and surrounding her with only those who loved her.

"Y'all ain't 'bout to do a damn thang to her. Evil bitches!" Krystal marched her way through the circle and grabbed Bonita's trembling hand. "If you even think about it I'ma tell my brother to beat you up after school," Krystal threatened.

All the girls were very familiar with her brother, Quincy, also known as Q. He had terrorized each of them on separate occasions as well as in groups. None of the girls dared mess with Krystal or anyone she befriended, because they didn't want to deal with Q taking their lunch money or pulling their hair and putting spit balls in it during the school day. They really hated when he smacked them on their butts as hard as he could. The sting would last for at least an hour.

"I didn't know that was yo' friend, Krystal. I'm not in this," one girl said and quickly made her way across the play ground. She was glad she left when she did once she saw Q approaching the circle of girls.

WHAPP!

Q smacked the leader of the pack on her butt as hard as he could as he infiltrated the circle. "Who messin' wit' my sista?" Q stared at each girl then jerked his shoulders out, making all of them jump back.

The girls didn't even bother responding; they all scattered, leaving only Krystal, Bonita and Quincy standing.

"What's yo' name?" Q asked Bonita.

"Bonita," she responded shyly, looking down at her feet. "Thanks for helping me. My house is right up the block... you can come over and play after school if you want to," Bonita said to Krystal, trying desperately to ignore Q staring at her.

"Okay," Krystal responded.

From that day on Krystal and Bonita were together every single day. Up until the day Krystal was murdered thirteen years later at the age of twenty-one.

Bo smiled at the memory before pulling up in Q's driveway. She rolled her eyes when she saw a shirtless Q posted up at the side door smoking a blunt, the butt of his gun hanging from his waistband.

"What up doe?! Hurry up, girl. You my partna," Q said as Bo approached the door.

"I told yo' ass I wasn't trying to play no spades, nigga. I'm tired as hell. I just want you to drop me off at home," protested Bo.

Entering the house, Bo saw two guys and a girl sitting at the dining room table. A third and more familiar guy was standing behind the girl, with a cup in one hand and a Newport in the other. A fifth of 1738 sat on the counter unopened, another half empty bottle sat on the table. Three blunts were in rotation. Bo fanned in front of her face as she walked into the living room, bypassing the entrance to the dining room.

"Come meet my peeps, Bonita." Q grabbed her arm and led her in the dining room.

All conversation stopped and Bo had everyone's full attention as she hesitantly walked in the room.

"This Bonita, y'all," Q said, breaking the silence. "These my cousins from Las Vegas, Lucky and Vegas," he said pointing to the two guys sitting at the table. "This Shenice… and you probably remember my cousin Rio. He used to come up here for the summer some times back in the day."

"Hi," Bo said before turning on her heels and heading out the room and back into the living room, where she sat on the couch and looked in her purse for her cell phone.

"I thought you was playing spades," Q yelled. Q and Rio walked in the living room.

"I told you I was trying to chill!"

"Play with them, Q. I'll chill with Bonita," Rio offered.

"I'm not trying to chill with you," Bo said with attitude. "Q, I'll just bring you your truck tomorrow. I'm out of here." Bo attempted to rise from the couch when Rio stood in front of her.

"Oh, you fucking Q? My bad," Rio apologized. He knew that wasn't the case from prior conversations with Q. He'd always had a thing for Bonita and was happy that once again destiny had placed her in his presence.

Bo's face screwed up. "I ain't fucking Q. You need to get out my way and stay the fuck out my business, Rio." Bo stood up expecting Rio to get out the way. When he didn't move, it caused them to stand so close Bo had to place her hands flat on his chest to prevent standing chest to chest with him. Before she could push him back, Rio grabbed her by each wrist.

"Why you so mean? I don't remember you being so fucked up back when I used to see you and Krystal outside jumping rope every day. You used to be the shy, little, cute girl. When you turn into such a bitch?" Rio calmly asked.

"Q, get yo' cousin off me... okay? Get him off me right now."

Q stepped between the two. "Chill out y'all. Bonita, go chill in my room for a minute, and I'll take you to the crib, okay?"

Bonita backed out the living room, never taking her eyes off Rio. She bumped into the wall before turning around and walking down the hall to Q's room.

Rio and Q laughed until Bo turned around and gave them the evil eye, causing the laughter to stop.

"Dawg, yo' girl something else. What's up with her?" Rio asked.

"She just had a bad day... she good people for real. I been trying to holla at her since before Krystal died and she won't give me no play."

"You ain't *never* hit that?" Rio looked like he didn't believe Q.

"Naw... well... I a- ain't never hit that, man." Q started to tell Rio about the incident that occurred, but was too embarrassed to admit he ate the pussy and still didn't get any.

"I'm on that." Rio shook his head up and down while biting his bottom lip.

Q wanted to tell him Bo was off limits, but he was certain she would never fuck with Rio anyway. "Do you, dawg. I give up on it. She say I'm like her brother anyway." Q walked back in the dining room and grabbed the blunt from Vegas. "I guess we're partners," he said to Shenice.

"Well sit yo' ass down and let's play then," Shenice replied, taking a long gulp of her drink.

Rio walked down the hall and entered Q's room without knocking. Upon entering, he found Bo staring at a blown up picture of herself, Q and Krystal. The picture was taken at Krystal's twenty-first birthday party; one week before she was murdered. In the picture they were all dressed up and had glasses of champagne in their hand.

Bo jumped when she heard the door open. Seeing it was Rio she exhaled loudly. "Look, I really am not in the mood for this. So please just leave me alone."

"I just wanted to apologize for messing with you earlier. It's good to see you again, Bonita," replied Rio, making his way over toward her. "Damn, I miss Krystal." He looked at the picture and held back tears. Unsuccessful in his attempt, a single tear escaped and made its way down his left cheek.

Bo looked over at Rio, taking in his appearance for the first time tonight. Rio was 6' 2" tall and 240 pounds. He was light-skinned with no facial hair but had a head full of hair he kept braided straight to the back. His bushy eyebrows reminded Bo of the rapper/actor/mogul Ice Cube's eyebrows, adding to Rio's already menacing look.

"I miss her, too," Bo said, allowing a tear of her own to escape.

Rio brushed the tear away with the back of his hand. "What you miss about her the most?"

Bo exhaled. "Everything... talking with her... hanging out... getting into shit." Bo laughed. "She was my sister... the only friend I ever had."

"I remember that time y'all told Q y'all had a new Vegas connect and got him to fly y'all out there to pick up a brick. I tried to tell that nigga y'all couldn't get no brick for $10,000. He called me mad as hell talking 'bout 'these bitches took my money and flew to Vegas to see the Mayweather/Judah fight!' He was really mad when I told him I saw y'all at the fight and gave y'all some VIP passes to the Mayweather after party."

"I remember that! Krystal said she was taking me to Vegas for my birthday to see the fight. I thought she was just talking, but once she told me her plans I was all in. We had so much fun in Vegas."

Rio stared into Bo's eyes. "You remember when we—"

"What happens in Vegas stays in Vegas," Bo said, cutting him off.

Rio chuckled. "Can we start over? I never forgot you. Why didn't you want me to—" The door flew open, making Rio stop talking mid-sentence.

"What up doe?" Q looked at Bo then Rio then back at Bo again. "You ready?"

"I can take you home right quick," Rio offered.

"I'm okay. I actually could use a drink. I'll just chill over here for a little while, Q." Bo really wasn't in the mood to be alone.

Q was surprised by Bo's sudden mood change but didn't say anything about it. I'll grab you a shot of 1738," he said, exiting the room.

When Q returned, Bo and Rio were seated on the couch at the foot of his bed watching an episode of *I Love Money*. Q handed Bo her drink and offered her the blunt he was smoking. Bo accepted the blunt, took two pulls and passed it to Rio. Rio hit the blunt a few times then passed it back to Bo.

Q watched them pass the blunt back and forth for a minute or two before saying, "Well damn! Y'all just gon' take my blunt!"

"Nigga, go roll another blunt... let us chill for a minute," said Rio.

"You betta gon' back to Grand Rapids with that shit, dawg," Q said, exiting the room. He paused in the hallway, contemplating going back in the room. He thought better of it, not wanting to appear to be cock blocking, and continued on into the dining room to finish the Spades game.

Bo and Rio finished off the blunt and their drinks while watching *I Love Money*. Once the show went off, Rio left to go refresh their drinks and returned with a blunt tucked behind his ear. Bo was totally relaxed by this time. There weren't too many people she was comfortable around and Rio was one of the few.

"You straight?" Rio asked. He placed the drinks on the dresser then bent down and began removing Bo's shoes.

"Thanks, Rio. I might as well grab some of Q's sweats and get out of this dress."

Bo stood and began searching through Q's dresser drawers. She was shocked to see the purple diary that could only belong to one person—Krystal. She had been looking for the diary since the day Krystal was found, hoping it would hold a clue to what happened to her. Bo didn't say anything to Rio about the diary. She planned on stealing it the first chance she got. *What the fuck is Q doing with Krys' diary... and how the fuck did he get it?* Bo thought.

She grabbed a T-shirt from the drawer and a pair of hooping shorts from another. "I'll be back."

"Where you going?" asked Rio.

"Quit playing... I'm going in the bathroom to change." Bo chuckled. *Rio is still something else. I wonder if we could have been good together.* She thought.

"Girl, you know you don't have to go in the bathroom to change. I've seen you get dressed on more than one occasion."

"Don't front, Rio. You may have seen me get dressed twice, but definitely not more than that." Bo attempted to go over to the door leading to the bathroom.

Rio grabbed her arms, stopping her from moving. "Don't forget about when I was up here for the funeral," Rio reminded her. They both thought back.

Everyone knew how hard Bonita was taking Krystal's death, so after the funeral a few people went over to her house from the cemetery. Rio noticed Bonita had been gone for a while and searched the house trying to find her when he heard her in her bedroom.

"What the fuck, Krystal! Who the fuck did this to you? I can't do this! I can't do this without you, Krys!" Tears poured from Bonita's eyes as she pulled at her hair from the roots.

Rio interrupted Bonita's moment of insanity, walking into her room and locking the door behind him. "Bonita, stop!" He pulled her hands from her hair and held her tightly against his broad chest.

"Why, Rio? Why somebody do this to Krys? She ain't never did nothing to nobody. Who would do this?" Bonita could not stop the tears from falling. She didn't attempt to hold back as she cried in Rio's arms.

"We gon' find out who did this to Krystal and I'm gon' kill them personally," Rio assured her.

"Promise me, Rio."

"I promise, Bonita. Q and I gon' handle this." Rio kissed her on the forehead softly. "I'm here for you, baby. I'm not gon' let you leave me again. I'm not gon' let anything happen to you."

Bonita began to kiss Rio. She wanted to forget this day ever happened. She wanted to forget Krystal was dead. She wanted to forget her parents were dead. She wanted to forget she was all alone in this world. She felt comfort in Rio's strong arms.

Before they knew what was happening, Rio and Bonita were in her bed sexing like they had been doing it for years instead of for the third time. Rio was slow stroking Bonita while softly sucking on her ear, driving her crazy in the process. He hadn't forgotten how that drove her crazy when they were in Vegas.

As they were basking in the afterglow of great sex, Rio asked Bonita if she wanted him to move down to Detroit or if she was coming to Grand Rapids. She was supposed to think about it and let him know, but weeks later she called and told him she'd changed her mind and just wanted to be left alone.

Rio was furious after several attempts to contact Bonita only to discover her number was disconnected and she had moved. He'd tried to get Q to tell him where she was at, but Q wouldn't budge. Rio had promised Bonita he wouldn't tell Q anything about them, so over a period of time he just gave up.

This was around the time Bonita became Bo and separated herself from the few people who were still in her life—with the exception of Q. This was the first time Rio had seen Bonita since then.

Rio grabbed the shorts and bent down to assist Bonita with putting them on. He unzipped her dress in the back and slid it down then put the T-shirt over her head. "You want me to find you some socks?"

"Yeah, thanks." Bonita sat back down on the couch. She glanced over at the drawer that held Krystal's diary then grabbed her drink from the dresser.

Rio put the socks on her feet then grabbed his drink. He turned the TV to an R&B music station and lit the blunt. The two reminisced while getting fucked up until they passed out on the couch.

Q entered his bedroom to find Bo and Rio passed out. Rio was sitting up with his head cocked to the left resting slightly on top of Bo's. Bo had her feet curled up under her and her head rested on Rio's chest. Q was surprised, but figured they must have got fucked up and just passed out. It looked innocent enough, so he didn't think twice about it.

He noticed Bo had changed clothes and immediately looked in the drawer for Krystal's diary. Finding it untouched, Q breathed a sigh of relief. He grabbed the diary and quickly stashed in under his mattress then exited the room just as quietly as he had come in.

CHAPTER 7

"What's up, Bonita," Rio asked.

"How did you get my number?" responded Bo.

"I got it out yo' phone when you went to sleep the other night. Don't be mad, but I knew you would pull some disappearing acts shit. I don't know what's up with you and Q, but that nigga ain't giving up shit when it comes to you." Passing Hart Plaza, Rio cruised down Jefferson in a burgundy 2008 Chevy Trailblazer SS. Living in Grand Rapids, he never purchased luxury vehicles, because the police would be on him.

Bo didn't bother cursing him out, because he had the number now. She had woke up early in the morning and looked in the drawer for Krystal's diary, but it wasn't there. She was beginning to think she was just buzzing and imaging things last night. "What do you want, Rio? I'm kinda in the middle of something." Bo glanced over at the frightened bound and gagged female sitting on the loveseat in her small apartment.

"We need to talk. You already know what's up. I need some answers and I'm not leaving until I get them."

"Hold on. I got another call." Bo clicked over without looking at the caller ID. "Hello."

"I've been waiting on your call for over a week now," Chris calmly spoke. "Am I supposed to just forget about our relationship, Bonita?"

"I can't talk right now. I'm going to have to call you back." Bo clicked back over to Rio without saying goodbye to Chris. "I need to call you back."

"No, just meet me at Southern Fires. How long before you can be three?" asked Rio.

"I can't make it today. Just call me back, okay?"

"Be there in an hour, Bonita. I'll be waiting on you." Rio hung up.

Bo placed the phone back in her pocket. She shook her head, rolling her eyes as she tried to get back focused on the task at hand.

The woman on the loveseat was thirty-two year old Melinda Jefferson; who just happened to be caught up in somebody else's mess. She knew she had no business messing around with a seventeen-year-old boy for the pass month, but the lure of the money, status and the mind blowing sex she just couldn't refuse. Hell, she had a seventeen-year-old daughter herself that she hadn't seen or heard from since she left the same apartment two years ago—finally fed up with Melinda's trifling ways and determining she could do better out in the streets on her own.

Melinda met Mark during one of her daily trips to the corner store for a pack of Newports, a bag of Better Made plain chips and a two liter Vernors. She noticed the shiny new money green Range Rover from a block away as she approached the store. She was glad she'd taken the extra time to put on make-up and the short jean skirt and halter top she was wearing with four inch stiletto heels. Her hair and nails were also freshly done, so she was full of confidence when she stepped inside the store.

Mark never knew what hit him as Melinda seduced him with a sexy sway of her hips. Mark ignored the cashier telling him his total as he quickly turned his head in Melinda's direction. "Damn," he said out loud.

Melinda grabbed the chips and pop and sashayed over to the cashier. "I need a pack of Newports in the box," she said as she peeped Mark staring at her.

Mark still had not paid for his purchases. "Uh, put her stuff on my bill, too," he told the cashier, who was losing her patience.

"Thank you... I'm Melinda, but everybody around here calls me Me-Me. And you are..."

"Uh, Mark," he stammered. He could tell she was much older than he was, but the confidence his new found wealth and status gave him provided him with the needed courage for him to continue. "You, ummm... lookin' real good, Me-Me. Can you sing like Mariah?" Mark's age showed as he tried to step to Melinda.

Melinda was a gold digger from back when they were called sack chasers. She knew she could easily manipulate the young boy by throwing the pussy on him like she knew the young girls he messed with could never do. "My apartment is right up the street. I can show you better than I can tell you," she flirted, grabbing the bag with her stuff in it. "What's your name again, daddy?"

"Um... I'm Mark. Put a pack of those Magnums on there too," he told the cashier as the line behind him continue to grow with impatient customers who dared not say a word to Mark in fear. At seventeen, Mark had the block on lock and was known to handle anyone who tried to get in the way of his money.

Mark paid for the purchases and grabbed his bag. Melinda followed him out the door. She paused when she got outside, not sure if he was really coming to her place or not.

"You wit' it... right?" Mark asked as he hit the chirp on his car alarm.

"You know it, daddy," replied Melinda as she hurried over to the passenger side of the Range Rover. "You're gonna have to excuse my place. I don't have nobody to help me out. I'm barely paying the rent. I know you're used to living like a king. As a matter of fact... that's what I'm gonna call you from now on, King. Will you help me out, King?" Melinda got straight to the point during the short ride to her apartment.

Mark just listened. He was flattered that someone who looked as good as Melinda and was much older than him would actually be on *his dick so hard. I can't wait to show this fine bitch off at Belle Isle, he thought as he parked the truck. "I got you."*

Mark got out the truck and looked around before grabbing at his Glock 19 9mm. He chirped the alarm on the truck and followed Melinda in the door leading into the apartment building, watching her ass switch hard as she led the way.

That day Melinda freaked Mark in everyway imaginable. She licked and sucked and allowed him to fuck her in every hole she had. After she'd fucked him good, she fixed him a meal of fried pork chops, mashed potatoes, sweet corn and gravy. She even made a gallon of tropical punch Kool-Aid with lemon wedges in it. After fucking and sucking him some more she hit him up for $300, which he gladly gave her before finally leaving, completely satisfied and anticipating the next time he'd see her.

Melinda and Mark had been fucking every day since then. Each time he would give Melinda a few hundred dollars for whatever she said she needed it for. Mark knew she was playing him like a trick, but as good as she was treating him, he really didn't give a fuck. The money was nothing to a boss like him.

Mark had the best connect ever, a kid with connections in Columbia. Mark started out getting ten keys at a time for $75,000. That was eleven months ago and now he was getting a hundred keys at a time for half a mill. Money definitely was nothing to him.

"I need you to come see me, King. I have a surprise for you." Melinda tried to hide the terror in her voice while doing as Bo had instructed her to do after pulling down the gag.

"What's up, Me Me? I was just over there last night. What you need now?" Mark made a U-turn as he spoke into the phone. His dick jumped at the though of fucking Me-Me in the ass. He ignored the change in her voice as he thought about fucking the hell out of her.

"I just need you to come over here right now." Melinda stared at the gun pointed directly at her forehead and shook in fear.

Bo stood over Melinda with her bottom lip tucked in. She had been trying to catch Mark slipping for a week with no luck. She finally decided to get him at Melinda's when Q started pressing her about getting it done. Bo made a throat slashing motion, telling Melinda to cut the conversation.

"I'll be waiting on you, King... so hurry up." Melinda ended the call. "Can I leave now? I did everything you told me to do." Melinda began to cry. She had started seeing moments in her life flash by.

"Not until Mark gets here. Just sit tight and don't try nothing stupid and you will be fine. Now shut the fuck up," Bo said as she replaced the gag and moved Melinda to the small bedroom.

Twenty minutes later, there was a knock at the door. Bo looked over at Melinda and spoke in a whisper. "If you want to live I'm telling you not to try and scream or do any dumb shit. I'm here for Mark, but you can get it too if you cause trouble for me. Once I take care of Mark I'll leave, but I know where you live, so don't even think about going to the police," Bo gave Melinda false hope.

"I swear I won't say a word. Please... just don't hurt me," Melinda begged through the gag.

Bo walked over to the door with her right hand behind her back, concealing her weapon. "Who is it?" she asked in a girly voice.

"Umm... King... uh... Mark."

Bo opened the door slowly. "Hi, sexy." She looked him up and down. "She ain't tell me you was this fine. You don't look like you can handle both of us," Bo teased.

Mark couldn't hide his shock as he stood in the doorway staring at the beautiful girl inside. "Umm... Uhh... A... ah," he mumbled incoherently.

"You're looking for Melinda, right?" Bo said sweetly.

"Yeah."

"Well come on in. We've been waiting on you. Melinda is in the bathroom right now." Bo turned to the side so he could enter. She nodded her head towards the living room, telling Mark to go ahead of her. "I want to check you out from the back, sexy." Bo smiled.

Mark walked toward the living room. He glanced back at Bo before taking a seat on the couch. "What you hiding," Mark asked jokingly. He'd noticed Bo had never removed her hand from behind her back.

"This is the deal, Mark," Bo said, coming from behind her back with the gun.

"What the fuck!" Mark jumped up from the couch and grabbed for his Glock.

"Don't do that, Mark!" Bo yelled, her trigger finger quivering.

Mark grabbed the handle of the Glock and was pulling it out when he heard a wizzing sound then felt a sharp burning pain in his chest. The Glock fell from his hand, hitting the floor as he grabbed his chest and slid back down onto the couch.

Bo pounced on him, kicking the gun across the floor. "I told yo' ass not to fuckin' move... hard headed ass nigga."

"That bitch Me Me set me up," Mark said then spit blood out his mouth.

"No, actually Q wants you gone. You bad for his business... with yo' low ass prices, and you got the nerve to blame this on poor Melinda. You the one got her caught up in yo' bullshit."

Mark was flooding the city with the best cocaine it had seen since YBI. He had already stolen four of Q's main customers, digging deep into Q's pockets. Q wanted Mark dead simply to knock his hustle. He figured with Mark dead his money would start back flowing like it did before Mark got on.

Mark looked up at Bo in confusion. He began chocking on his blood. "I don't even fuck wit' Q." He gasped for air.

"Maybe you should have," Bo responded before delivering her customary forehead shot.

Heading over to the bedroom where a terrified Melinda awaited her fate, Bo actually felt bad for the girl. *Yeah, she had no business messing with a boy that age anyway, but is that a reason to die*, Bo thought. Bo entered the room and immediately put two slugs in Melinda's head.

As she headed back through the living room to make her exit, she heard Mark's cell phone begin to ring. *Just throw it in the bag. Ohh, ohhh; ohh, ohhh; ohh ohhh; just through it in the bag*. Bo cracked open the door and looked out. Once she saw the coast was clear she put the gun in her waistband, wiped down the doorknobs and quickly left the apartment building.

Bo headed to the black 2008 Nissan Maxima she had rented. Before she knew what she was doing, she jumped on I96 and headed toward downtown Detroit. Her cell phone rang, interrupting her thoughts.

"What up doe!" Q said before Bo could even say hello. "Is that handled?"

"Yeah, it's handled," Bo said dryly.

"Well let's go grab something to eat. Where you at?"

"Actually, I'm on my way to meet someone to get something to eat now. I'll holla at you later." Bo rushed to get off the phone.

"Wait! Who you meeting? Chris?" Q inquired.

"No. Um, I'm meeting Rio. I'll call you a little later."

"What's up with you and Rio? First you laid all up on this nigga sleep and now y'all dating? You tryin' to get with him?"

"Q, I'm not trying to get with Rio. He the one called and asked me to meet him. I don't even know what it's about. And I don't have to explain shit to you anyway. You not my man, so I wish you would quit acting like you are. Hello… hello. Mutha fucka!" Quincy had hung up on Bo in anger. She debated calling back, but decided to make him call her back first since he was the one who hung up on her.

𝔇

Bo parked on the street and walked through the parking lot and up the stairs to enter Southern Fires. She instantly spotted Rio, because the restaurant was strangely empty compared to how it was usually packed with hungry customers no matter the time or day of the week.

Rio approached Bo and embraced her tightly. He held her for what seemed like hours but was actually only a minute or two. *Damn this feels good. I don't even want to let her go*, Rio thought. He felt Bo pull back from him and grabbed her up even tighter. "I'm glad you came. I already got a table. Come on."

Rio let Bo out of his embrace and grabbed her hand, leading her over to a booth by the kitchen, in the back of the restaurant.

Bo glanced around the mostly empty restaurant. She inconspicuously squeezed her purse, instantly reassured by the feel of the hard steel. She was glad she didn't leave her gun in the car.

"So… I finally get my time to talk with the infamous Bonita," Rio said as they sat.

"What... infamous... what the hell you talking about, Rio?" Bo wrinkled her brow. She hoped Q hadn't been talking about her with Rio.

"I'm just saying. Not only have you managed to brush me off one time, but you actually had the rare opportunity to do it twice."

"Hey... I'm Tamika and I'll be you're waitress. Can I get y'all something to drink?" the chubby, mocha colored girl asked.

"I think we're ready to order," Rio responded, nodding his head at Bo for her to order first.

"I'll have the smothered steak with mashed potatoes and gravy, greens, black eye peas and yams. I also want a coke and a caramel shake." Bo closed the menu and held it out to the waitress.

"You only get two sides with your dinner. The other two will—"

"I know," Bo cut her off. "What you getting?" She turned her attention to Rio.

"That sounds good what you ordered. I think I want the same thing and let me get a catfish dinner... oh, and a lemonade, too." Rio reached across the table and grabbed Bo's hand.

The waitress looked at them both then grabbed the other menu and took off to place their order. *Them some greedy ass mutha fuckas. They bet not think they 'bout to run the fuck outta me. Shit... Craig ass back in jail and I got the nerve to be pregnant again. Fuck, Ne-Yo ain't but one and he still ain't potty trained. I ain't got but two diapers left... I need to make some fuckin' money today,* Tamika thought as she put their order in. She glanced over at them once again before heading off to make their drinks.

"Okay, cut to the chase. What happened, Bonita?" Rio left his side of the table and moved to sit next to Bonita. "I was gon' move here to be with you. Why you disappear on me... twice?"

"I don't know." Bo looked around nervously. *What you want me to say? You want the truth? Okay, I can fall in love with you, Rio. We could move away and be happy together... but first I have to finishing killing people so I can make enough money to start a new life some where else. I'm a hit woman... I kill people for a living. Do you still love me? Huh, Rio... you still want to move here to be with me?* Bo thought but stopped after her first three words.

"Bonita. Bonita. What you mean you don't know? What kinda answer is that?" Rio snapped Bo out of her thoughts.

"It's the truth. I'm just... I'm a different person now, Rio."

"So am I, but I still feel the same way every time I see you."

"And how is that?"

"I feel like...," Rio paused as the waitress placed their drinks on the table.

"Make sure you bring me some A1 and some extra napkins," Bo said.

"And I'm gon' need some tarter sauce and hot sauce," Rio added.

"Okay," Tamika said, quickly leaving the table. *Oh, these mutha fuckas got me twisted. I swear I'm gon' go the fuck off if they don't leave me a tip. My mutha fuckin' feet been hurting all week, and these greedy mutha fuckas making me carry all this fuckin' food. I hate my fukin' life!!!* Tamika thought.

"I feel like you all I need in a woman. I would be happy coming home to you every night. I can take care of you. Put a couple of my pretty babies up in you." Rio laughed, looking at Bonita.

"I don't want no babies. I got a lot going on right now, Rio. Stuff I don't even want to talk about. So, what have you been up to?"

"I'm not gon' let you just brush me off again, Bonita. What's up? You got a man or something?"

"Not really. I just want to focus on work, and in a year I'm moving."

"Where you going?" Rio's brow wrinkled with interest.

"I don't even know. Just far away from here. I want to go somewhere and buy me a house... maybe open up a business or something."

"Let's do it now. Right now, Bonita. Let's just disappear right now," Rio said seriously.

"Boy! I want my own. I don't want to depend on a nigga to take care of me. Shit happens. I have to make sure I'm okay, because there's no guarantee somebody is going to be here for me." Bo thought about her parents.

Janice and Dale were a dream couple. They were high school sweethearts, both attending Mackenzie High School in Detroit. Dale was the captain of the basketball team as well as Class Valedictorian. Janice was the cheer team captain and just as smart as Dale, graduating 2nd in her class, right behind Dale who was 1st.

Janice found out she was pregnant with Bonita a month before graduation. Dale couldn't have been happier and immediately rented a house on Oakman Boulevard, a few blocks away from Mackenzie. Janice was happy to move right in. She had been in the foster care system since birth and never knew her mother or father. Dale lived with his father. His mother passed away when he was ten. His father worked so many shifts at Chrysler it took him a month to realize Dale had moved out.

They both were determined to graduate high school and attend college. Dale was sure he could make this happen, because not only was he a star basketball player with many colleges scouting him, he was also a very prosperous drug dealer. He had been selling ya-yo since ninth grade and was stacking most of his money.

Dale eventually signed to play ball with Michigan State, but was injured in the high school state playoffs and never made it to MSU.

He decided to focus on his other passion… drugs. He was good at selling drugs and loved the freedom it afforded him. He planned to use his brain to get over in the streets and maybe go to college later on in life.

As the years went by, Dale and Janice lived what appeared to be a perfect life. They both had nice cars. They took a vacation every year. Their baby had everything a child could ever want. She was her mother's princess and daddy's little girl. The only thing they ever argued about was their living arrangements. They were still renting the same house on Oakman Boulevard, and Janice wanted to move to the suburbs. Dale refused to leave the hood and have the police harass him every time he came home. That would ultimately be part of their downfall.

The day Bonita found her parents dead in her home was forever imprinted in her mind. It was a day she would never forget. It was the last day of her tenth grade year. She had run all the way home to pack her overnight bag so she could head over to Krystal's house. She secretly hoped Krystal's cousin Rio came over to spend the night as well.

Bonita immediately knew something was wrong when she got home and the door was cracked open. The driveway was empty, which was also rare. Someone was always there to greet her when she got home from school.

"Mama… daddy," Bonita screamed, entering the house to find it ransacked.

She saw her mother first. She was lying on her back in the entryway between the living room and dining room with gunshot wounds to her chest. In her right hand was a small silver gun.

"Oh my God!! Mama!" Bonita kneeled down at her mother's side and cried. "Who did this, Mama?! Who did this?!"

Bonita heard a gurgling sound coming from the kitchen and ran to investigate. There she found her father lying face down with three bullet holes in his back and blood flowing from his mouth as he choked.

"Daddy! Daddy!" She rushed over and flipped his body so he lay on his back. "Who did this, Daddy?! Who killed Mama?" Bonita was screaming hysterically, her face soaked with tears.

"I'm sorry, baby. Daddy and Mama... love you so much," he said between chokes. "Go in my room... look in the closet under the floor."

"I have to call 9-1-1, Daddy." Bonita turned to leave the room but stopped when her father called her name.

"Bonita... it's too late, baby."

"Nooooo! Daddy! Who did this to you? What am I going to do now, daddy? Where will I go? Who is going to take care of me?"

"Quincy." Blood splattered on the floor as he coughed. "Q."

"Daddy, I'm calling 9-1-1!" Bonita looked into her father's eyes and saw them roll back in his head. "No, Daddy! Nooooo!" she yelled.

Bonita held her father in her arms and cried for at least an hour. After kissing her father's cheek she slowly got up, her clothes now soaked in her father's blood. As she headed to her parent's room she stopped at her mother's body.

"I love you sooo much, Mommy." She bent down and kissed her mother's cheek. Bonita hesitated before grabbing the gun from her mother's hand and heading upstairs to her parent's bedroom.

She ran straight to the closet and noticed nothing looked disturbed. After moving all the shoes on the floor she felt around for a way to remove the floorboard. After several minutes, she finally got them removed and saw a small black duffel bag. She grabbed the bag then quickly headed into her bedroom.

Once inside her room, she grabbed her luggage and began to pack as much of her stuff as she could. At this moment she couldn't think. All she could do was move. Hearing the door slam shut, she stopped moving and listened closely. She could hear movement downstairs. She grabbed the gun from her dresser and moved behind the door.

"Bonita! What the fuck!" Krystal shouted. She had just spotted Bonita's mother on the floor.

"Damn, where is Bonita?" Quincy ran up the stairs full speed, yelling Bonita's name.

Realizing it was Q, Bonita ran out her room and met him at the top of the stairs. "Somebody killed my parents." She rushed into Q's arms, still crying hysterically.

"Are you alright?" he asked.

"Yeah… my dad told me to come to you. He told me to get his money and go… right before he died."

"Come on," Q grabbed her arm and led her into her bedroom.

"What is going on?" Krystal asked as she made her way up the stairs.

"Somebody killed her mom and dad," Q answered.

"Who?"

"We don't know, Krystal. Just help her get her stuff so she can get out of here."

Quincy left the girls to pack Bonita's things. He went in her parent's room and looked around. After finding a large rolling luggage, he began to fill it with all of Bonita's parent's valuables. He ran downstairs, passing both bodies, and headed down to the basement. After searching for a while, he finally found a large bag filled with ya-yo and three guns. He headed back upstairs and put everything in the luggage then went in Bonita's room where the girls were just finishing up.

Quincy grabbed one of the three suitcases Bonita had packed and headed downstairs carrying a suitcase in each had. Krystal grabbed one of the suitcases and headed out the room.

"Come on, Bonita. Let's go," Krystal said sadly.

Stopping at the door, Bonita looked around her room. She propped the suitcase she was carrying up against the wall and went over to her nightstand to retrieve a picture of her and her parents on an outing to Cedar Point. She placed the picture in her blood stained purse and headed out the door with Krystal leading the way.

Krystal's grandmother called the police and told them what happened once the kids told her. There was an investigation, but no one was ever charged with the murders. Bonita lived with Krystal and her grandmother from that day up until her and Krystal moved into their own place just weeks before Krystal was murdered. Quincy came around daily, but didn't really live at his grandmother's house.

"You be zoning out, girl. I think you need to be taken care of... you so... so intense. You need a vacation. Let's go somewhere."

Bonita snapped out of it and looked over at Rio. "I'm sorry. I got a lot on my mind."

"I see. That's why you need to let me take you away for a few days. Let's go to Mexico," Rio said, rubbing Bo's shoulders as he spoke.

"I'm not interested in going to Mexico, Rio. I'm trying to tell you I got a lot going on."

"A lot like what, Bonita. Where do you even work at?"

Bonita was happy the waitress came over with their food.

"Anything else?" the waitress asked after placing all the plates on the table.

"Nope, we good," Rio answered, excusing her.

I swear I'ma quit this job and start stripping as soon as I lose twenty-five pounds, Tamika thought as she walked away.

"This all looks so good," Bonita said, changing the subject.

"Yeah... enjoy your food, but don't think I'm giving up on getting you outta town and to myself." Rio picked up a piece of catfish and bit it. He shuffled it around in his mouth to prevent burning himself. "This shit is hot as hell."

Bonita laughed at him as she put A1 on her steak and butter on her cornbread. *Maybe having Rio in my life again isn't such a bad thing after all. Maybe I should just give him a chance. I don't know what to do*, Bo thought as she ate her food and listened to Rio try to convince her to go out of town with him.

CHAPTER 8

Weeks had passed since Bo's dinner with Rio. She couldn't believe she was actually packing. Rio wasn't successful in talking her into going to Mexico, but she did agree to go to an overnight stay at a place of Rio's choice. She was nervous but excited as well. Rio had been calling her daily. She was actually happy to have someone to talk to every day again, since she hadn't been taking Chris' calls.

She'd already successfully completed her two hits scheduled for today. Carmen Foster, a thirty-something female that worked at a downtown lawyer's office was her first hit. Carmen's husband wanted her dead so he could collect on the $250,000 insurance policy she stupidly placed on herself to make sure he would be all right if something ever happened to her. Thomas Gross, a twenty-four-year-old homo thug was her second hit. Ross Lester, a husband, father and Thomas' secret lover, placed the hit on Thomas to keep his secret from his wife when Thomas threatened to tell it all if Ross didn't leave his wife for him.

Bo waited patiently in the bathroom dressed as a maintenance worker while pretending to fix the toilet in the last stall. When Carmen entered the bathroom the first two times during the day someone else was in there as well. Bo waited for the perfect opportunity to strike and finally got it after waiting four hours.

The third time Carmen entered the rest room it was empty, with the exception of Bo. Bo knew she was pressed for time, so she struck quickly. As Carmen made her way to the first stall, Bo followed her. Once Carmen realized Bo was right up on her, it was too late.

"This one's from your greedy ass husband," Bo said, shooting Carmen twice in the back of the head at point blank range.

Carmen fell face first into the toilet bowl, causing a loud bang and a splash. Bo quickly placed her gun in the pocket on the front of her apron then grabbed her tool box and exited the restroom. She pulled her hat down low over her eyes as she briskly walked toward the building's exit.

"Hey!" a woman called out as Bo put her hand on the handle of the door exiting the building. Bo turned around slowly, her hand automatically reaching for her weapon.

"You finally got that one toilet fixed, huh? You been here for hours so I know you're glad to finally be finished." The nosey lady had been to the bathroom six times that day and was in no rush to get back to her desk.

"Oh, I finished that one the last time you were in there. I've been working on the downstairs men's room since then," Bo answered, opening the door.

"Well have a great day," Ms. Nosey shouted out.

Bo exited the building without looking back. She knew she only had a few minutes to get out of the area before police would be everywhere. She was also running late to her next hit. She rushed over to the rental she had parked on the other side of the building and speed off.

Her next hit would be easier because she would have a key to get in his apartment. Ross informed her that a key to the apartment would be under the welcome mat and Thomas would be in the shower at one o'clock sharp. Thomas was expecting Ross at one-thirty and would be waiting butt naked in bed, lying on his stomach, as he was instructed to be.

Bo thought about her upcoming night with Rio as she drove to Thomas' house. She imagined Rio making love to her again. Her thoughts were interrupted by a call from Chris. She ignored the call and continued to think about Rio until she pulled up at Thomas' apartment. Thomas lived at Pebble Creek in Southfield. It was one of those apartments where you entered each townhouse individually.

Bo parked a few doors down and walked down to the apartment door. She looked around suspiciously before quickly bending down and retrieving the key from under the mat. There was a magnetic sign that said J.T's Cleaning Service on the side of the car, so Bo wasn't too worried about it still being light outside. Besides, she knew first hand that most people didn't even pay attention to what was happening right under their noses.

Bo entered the apartment and quietly headed up the stairs. Ross had already told her the layout of the place, so she knew exactly where she was headed. After clearing the stairs, she made a quick right and entered the bedroom. Her jaw dropped at the sight of a naked Thomas lying across the bed butt naked with a pillow up under him, propping his ass up high into the air.

"I'm ready for you, daddy," Thomas said in a feminine voice. He glanced back to look at Ross and was surprised to see Bo instead. "What the fuck!" Thomas said, attempting to grab the comforter to cover himself and sitting up. "Who the fuck is you?" Thomas' first thought was the intruder was Ross' wife. He soon found out that couldn't be further from the truth.

"Ross sent me," Bo replied. "He said you'd been making some threats."

"What!" Thomas smacked his glossy lips. "Bitch, if you don't get the fuck up outta my house I'ma—" Thomas stopped mid-sentence after seeing the shiny Glock Bo was now brandishing.

"You gonna what? You fake ass thug. I'm gonna enjoy this shit. You going around acting like you all hard and shit. Probably fucking females and not even telling them you fucking niggas too... then got the nerve to threaten to snitch on Ross. I need to kill both of y'all asses. Trifling ass niggas."

"Please... please don't shoot me," Thomas begged as he scooted up to the top of the bed. "I love Ross. Nobody understands us. Please don't kill me!"

Bo released two quick shots, the first entering Thomas' chest, the second entering his forehead. His body jerked back to the headboard before sliding down on the bed in a grotesque position. Bo searched the *apartment carefully. After coming up with only $300 she'd found stashed in the nightstand drawer, she left the apartment just as quickly as she'd come.*

Bo threw the last of her things in her luggage and dragged it down to the living room. She had insisted on meeting Rio at the room. He still didn't know where she lived and she wanted to keep it that way. As much as she hated to admit it, she had always felt Rio. But no matter what happened with him, she was still prepared to up and leave in 30 seconds. After stopping to think about everything she packed, she felt confident she wasn't forgetting anything. She grabbed her purse off the couch and rolled her luggage to the side door leading into the garage. Bo put her luggage in the trunk then hopped in the driver's seat of the rental. She pulled out the garage and headed towards the freeway, excited about what tonight would bring.

𝔇

Bonita smiled at Rio as she parked next to his truck at the Holiday Inn on Telegraph Road. She popped the trunk and stepped out the car. Rio jumped out his truck and rushed over to hug Bonita. He held her tightly for a few moments then kissed her softly on the forehead.

"You ready to go?" he asked as he broke his embrace and grabbed her suitcase out the trunk, placing it in his truck.

"Ready to go… we here, right?" Bonita asked, confusion wrinkling her brow.

"Well, actually… I want you to ride with me to the hotel so we can talk during the ride. You didn't think I was bringing you here… did you?"

"Where is this hotel at?"

"It's in Illinois, but it only takes about four hours to get there. You said you would stay overnight, and I'll make sure you home safe tomorrow night." Rio smiled at Bonita and grabbed her hands. "I need this time with you, Bonita. Just let me take you away from all your stress and pamper you for a day."

"I guess," Bo responded, hesitantly getting in Rio's truck.

Rio's smile was wide as he pulled out the parking lot and onto Telegraph Road. He glanced over at Bonita and smiled even wider.

"What you smiling at?" Bonita asked. "Don't make me jump up out this truck." She chuckled.

Rio accelerated. "You mine for the next twenty-four hours, sexy. You ain't going no where this time." Rio joined in her laughter. "What you been doing all day anyway," he asked.

"Handling a little business... what about you? What you do today?" Once again Bonita flipped the script.

"I hit a couple niggas up before meeting you. I been waiting on this all day though. I put some thought into this overnight trip, so I hope you appreciate it." Rio looked over at Bonita and winked.

"What the fuck is all that?" Bonita laughed. "I thought this trip was supposed to be all about de-stressing me."

"It is. I'ma make sure all that stress gone before we leave the room."

"Yeah right... I don't think it's possible for me not to be stressed. I'm ready to move for real."

"I told you I was down. Ain't shit in Grand Rapids. Where you trying to go?"

"I don't know... but wherever I go... I gotta go alone," Bonita said sadly.

"Why? Why you don't wanna fuck with me? I got a little something put up... you a be straight."

"I got problems, Rio... issues you can't even imagine. I thought you were supposed to be taking my mind off all that shit though?" Robin Thicke's "Complicated" played softly in the background.

"Shit, we all got problems. I can help you get rid of your problems. I need somebody I can trust. I ain't gotta be fucking five or six bitches. I'm good with just one bad ass ride or die. That's you, Bonita. No matter where we at I'm good... you good."

"You got some Young Jezzy up in here?" Bonita asked, grabbing a CD case from the middle console and flipping through it.

"Yeah, it's in there. You sho'll know how to spin a nigga, don't you. You won't tell me shit about you... you one of them mysterious ma-fuckas." Rio glance over at Bonita then switched lanes.

Bonita continued to flip through the CDs until she found *The Recession*. She put it in the CD player then leaned back in her seat and listened to the intro. The sun was shining brightly in her eyes, forcing her to dig her sunglasses out her purse and put them on.

They talked about everything yet nothing at all as they headed to I94 and continued to drive for four hours until they got to Illinois. Bonita tried her best to make Rio tell her where the hell they were going, but he wouldn't budge. He kept telling her it was a surprise.

Thirty minutes later, when they finally pulled up at Sybaris, Bonita still didn't know where she was at. She looked around at all the flowers and greenery surrounding the property. It looked like a small community of houses as opposed to a hotel.

"Where the hell you got me?" She threw a confused glance Rio's way.

"I'll be right back. Let me go check us in." Rio jumped out the truck and was quickly out of Bonita's sight.

"What the fuck have I gotten myself into now?" Bonita shook her head and turned around to glance out the back window. "Where the fuck this nigga got me at?" she said out loud. She pulled out her cell phone and checked to make sure she still had service. She was happy to see she did.

After nervously shifting in her seat for an additional ten minutes, Rio bounced back to the truck with some papers and a garage door opener in his hands and a big grin on his face. He jumped in the truck and took off without saying a word. Rio turned a few corners then stopped to open a garage before pulling into it.

The semi-lit garage prompted Bonita to place her hand in her purse so she could grip her gun. She sat in the truck while Rio jumped out and walked to the back of the truck to grab their bags then walked over and opened Bonita's door.

"Come on," he said, turning on his heels and walking out the garage and over to the door of the cottage.

Bonita cautiously followed Rio, her hand still gripping the gun in her purse. Her head swiftly moved from side to side as she scoped out her surroundings. She felt so out of her comfort zone. Like a sitting duck, waiting for the ambush. "I thought we were going to a hotel, Rio?"

"This is a hotel," he replied, opening the door and moving to the side so Bonita could enter.

Bonita was not prepared for the sight that lay before her. She actually gasped in surprise before stepping inside the tropical oasis. Upon entering, the lighting dimmed to a romantic setting. Mood music began to flow through a state of the art surround sound system. To her right was a swimming pool with a cascading waterfall and a slide.

Straight ahead and up seven stairs was a suite unlike any she had ever seen.

Bonita paused and looked over the wooden rails in the loft area down into the pool area. There was a scene of a tropical sunset with a palm tree on one wall and a mirror reflecting the pool on another. Two chairs sat inside a large shower/steam room. There were also two chairs and a table poolside. Large green plants were placed everywhere from the ceiling to each corner of the room and even on every ledge. A lighted border illuminated the top of the walls near the ceiling.

Rio walked past Bonita and placed their things near the bed. "So... what do you think?"

Bonita was speechless. She took in everything as she walked over to the bed. The spacious open floor plan featured a huge glass enclosed suite with mirrors everywhere. The headboard was all mirrors and there was even a lighted mirror on the ceiling above the bed. There was a see-through fire place with a cute table for two, holding a chilled bottle of champagne, next to it.

What Bonita really loved was the huge jucuzzi right next to the bed, which was also surrounded by mirrors. The room looked like it was made for lovers; lovers who held no inhabitations and wanted to put it all out there for the other to share and enjoy. Everything was out in the open.

"Um... what you say?" Bonita was so overwhelmed by the grandeur of the room she didn't even hear Rio's question.

Rio beamed inwardly, but kept a cocky swagger on the outside. "I said... do you like the room."

"It's beautiful. I can't believe how nice this is."

"Well get comfortable. I need to grab the cooler out the truck." Rio kissed Bonita on the forehead before heading back down the stairs and out the door.

Bonita walked out the bedroom and peered over the rail down at the pool. *Damn this room is nice. I wonder how much he paid for this room for the night*, she thought as she sat in a chair overlooking the pool. *I can not catch feeling for him under no circumstances. This is really romantic though.* Bonita exhaled loudly and relaxed her shoulders. She positioned her oversized purse on her lap and thought back to the time she spent with Rio in Vegas.

Bonita exited the restroom in the overcrowded Mayweather after party only to find Krystal rushing toward her, pissy drunk. The short royal blue dress Krystal wore crept up her thighs, giving a much welcome peek to the vultures who watched her every step, hoping to be the lucky guy to leave with her.

"Bonita! Bonita!" *Krystal screamed as she got closer to Bonita.*

"Girl, you fucked up!" *Bonita laughed at her girl when she saw how drunk she really was.* "C'mon. I'm taking your ass right to the room."

"Un unh... nope!" *Krystal danced around doing an exaggerated version of the cabbage patch, causing Bonita to pull down her dress, which was now exposing her bare ass cheeks.*

"Girl! Bring your ass on! We're leaving before you do some stupid shit." *Bonita's attempt to pull Krystal toward the exit was unsuccessful.*

Krystal's body stiffened as she stopped to explain the exuberant mood she was in. "Remember when I told you I was not leaving Vegas without seeing what Floyd Mayweather was working with!" *she shouted above Ne-Yo's "Sexy Love."*

"Yeah! You got that nigga?!" *Bonita was excited for her, because what girl didn't think Mayweather was sexy as hell, and his swag was second to none.*

"Naw." *Krystal giggled.* "But I'm 'bout to leave with," *she leaned to the side and squinted her eyes before finishing,* "umm... Michael Jones. He staying at our hotel in room 2014. Here." *Krystal handed Bonita a balled up napkin.*

Bonita opened the napkin and read: Michael Jones room 2014 - 15 Via Mantova, Henderson, NV 89011. "What the hell is this? And what the hell Mayweather got to do with this guy?"

"His address and nothing. I'm just horny as hell, so I'm gon' act like this nigga is Mayweather!" Krystal laughed hysterically.

"So you just gon' ditch me for some dick? And how you know this not a fake address?"

"Hell yeah, and I checked his license and social security card. Go hang with Rio… he's over at that bar." Krystal pointed to where Rio was standing with another guy, both with a bottle of champagne in their hand.

"Okay… be careful." Bonita hesitantly placed the napkin in her purse.

"Don't do nothing I wouldn't do," Krystal shouted over "It's Goin' Down" by Young Joc as she staggered over to a cocky black guy wearing a business suit.

Bonita shouted back, "Well that leaves the door wide open!" On the low, Bonita was horny as hell, too. She walked over to the bar where Rio stood drinking champagne from the bottle.

"Ya girl left you for a nigga, huh?" Rio was watching as it all went down. "You can hang out with me. You wanna go gamble?"

"No. I think I'm going back to the room and chill out." Bonita yawned, resisting the urge to use Rio to satisfy her needs.

"Can I go with you? What happens in Vegas stays in Vegas." Rio allowed the champagne to supplement his cockiness. He took a long swig from the bottle then leaned in close to Bonita and softly kissed her neck.

The feel of Rio's lips on her neck made Bonita's level of horniness reach a point she couldn't return from without his help. "You can't tell Krys or Q. Naw, you can't tell nobody. I'm serious, Rio. You can't tell nobody… I'm talkin' 'bout nobody." Bonita sang like Aaliyah.

Surprised by her reaction, Rio wasted no time. He placed the bottle on the bar then grabbed her hand and headed for the exit. He had been waiting as long as he could remember to get Bonita alone in a room.

"Hey, man. What's up?" the guy standing next to Rio asked. He threw his hands in the air, spilling champagne on a lady standing next to him. She glanced over at him but didn't make a fuss about it.

"Change of plans. I'll call you tomorrow," Rio yelled without looking back or slowing his stride.

"I'm serious, Rio. You better not tell anyone," Bonita threatened.

"I'm not. If I tell I know you won't give me no mo'. So I ain't saying shit. Unless it's garbage... then I'm tellin' everybody!" Rio laughed.

"Boy, quit playing! I'm serious!" Bonita punched him lightly in the arm.

As soon as they got in the room all clothes hit the floor. Bonita pushed him over to the oversized chair and straddled him. Rio gripped her ass as they grinded against each other and tongue-kissed like love sick teenagers. When he just couldn't take it any more, Rio lifted Bonita up and positioned her over his erect penis.

"Ohhhhh," Bonita moaned loudly. Rio wasn't the first guy she ever slept with—those bragging rights belonged to the twenty-three year old molester named Patrick, also known as Milo, who had lured her over to his house when she was only fifteen and tricked her out of the pussy—but Rio was the largest guy she had ever slept with—at ten inches soft.

"Oh... oh... oh... oh... oh... oh... oh," Rio whimpered each time Bonita slid off his dick. She was only going half way down and the shit still felt good as hell to Rio. He tried to suck her titties while concentrating on not cumming too soon. When he felt his orgasm building, he lifted Bonita off his lap and positioned her over the ottoman in a doggie style position.

Bonita was in a daze. She couldn't believe she was fucking Rio. What would Krys think? She didn't have long to think before her thoughts were instantly brought back to reality when Rio slide inside her.

"*Awwwwwh! Slow down!*" Bonita yelled. *She could feel Rio's big balls slapping hard against her ass as he held her waist tight and pounded her.* "*Dang, nigga! Make me feel good, too!*"

"*I'm sorry.*" *Rio paused to catch his breath. His sweat-drenched body gleamed. While placing a trail of hot kisses down the middle of Bonita's back, he reached down and stroked her, using two fingers to apply pressure to her clit in a circular motion.*

"*That feels good,*" *Bonita moaned, responding to his touch by rolling her hips.* "*Ouuuuuuu, yeah... like that,*" *she coached him.*

Rio continued to kiss her neck and back while slowly rotating his hips to maneuver his way in. The juices from Bonita pussy made it hard for him to restrain himself, but he managed to do just that and slow stroked Bonita until she had an orgasm.

They ended up fucking for hours, breaking only to get something to drink and to allow Rio to get back hard. They fucked from the chair to the floor to the bed, in every way imaginable; until they passed out.

What seemed like minutes later, Bonita woke up to a ringing cell phone. "*Hello,*" *she said sleepily into the phone.*

"*Girl, get yo' ass up! You bet not have no niggas in the room.*" *Krystal laughed loudly.* "*I'm almost there.*"

"*Okay, bye!*" *Bonita hung up the phone.* "*Rio! Rio! Get up!*" *she yelled as she viciously shook Rio out of his sleep.*

"*What the fuck! What's up?!*" *Rio looked around the room as if he expected something to be going on.*

"*Krys is on her way to the room! You gotta get out of here!*" *Bonita jumped up and was grabbing Rio's things and throwing them at him.* "*Hurry up!*"

"*Damn! Okay!*" *Rio slid his boxers and wife beater on then ducked to prevent being hit with one of his shoes.*

Krystal's loud voice could be heard singing the song that was playing when Floyd Mayweather walked out to the ring. "*I'll whip your head boy... your ass could get killed. Two niggas in the front, two niggas in the back; that's four niggas ridin' strapped in grandpa's*

Cadillac. The voice in my head say fuck all these niggas. Then I start thinkin', I should rob all these niggas."

"She's here!" Bonita said in a hushed tone. "Get your stuff and get in the closet! Hurry up!" She continued to gather Rio's things and ran to toss them in the closet. Seeing Rio wasn't following her to the closet, she ran back and began to push him toward it.

"Come on—"

Rio was abruptly cut off when Bonita's hand flew over his mouth. "You promised you wouldn't tell," she whispered. They could hear Krystal fumbling with the room key at the door.

"Okay," Rio whispered, reluctantly stepping inside the closet just in the nick of time.

"It smells like sex up in here!" Krystal said swinging the door open wide. She was always a breath of fresh air, and today was no exception.

Realizing she was butt naked, Bonita ran over to the bed and wrapped a sheet around her. "Girl, please... ain't shit up." She tried to play it off.

"Ahhhhhh! You up in here fucking somebody!" Krystal ran over to the bed and bent down to look under it. "Who up in here?!" she continued to shout, running over to the bathroom and opening the door wide.

"Girl! Ain't nobody up in here. Okay... I was masturbating," Bonita lied with ease.

"Hell naw! Everybody do that shit, girl. You playing!" Krystal headed into the bathroom and shut the door.

Bonita shot over to the closet and rushed Rio out the room, half naked.

"I'ma call you later on today," he whispered as he shuffled out the door, dropping a sock in the process. He quickly kissed Bonita on the lips then the forehead and headed down to his room.

Krystal later found the sock and tried her best to get Bonita to confess, but she never did tell the truth.

"Are you hungry yet?" Rio asked. He'd entered the suite and was taking things out the cooler and placing them in the refrigerator.

"I'm still trying to get over this room. This is really beautiful." Bo stood up and walked over to Rio.

"Yeah, I ran across it on the humble. I was coming back home from outta town and stopped to get a room. They start explaining the membership fees and asking me if I needed a room with a pool in it, and I had to see this shit for myself. I only been here twice though. I usually get the Paradise suite, but this one is better." Rio began to warm containers of food in the microwave.

"Don't be bringing me where you take all your hoes." Bonita rolled her eyes.

"I said this room is better. You know you my special ho," Rio joked.

Bonita slapped him up side his head before giggling. "Come here," she said seductively.

"No."

"What you mean no?"

"No means no," Rio continued to joke. "Come here." Rio led Bonita over to the massage chair in the bedroom. He grabbed her purse from her, after a brief struggle, then hit some buttons on the chair and started it. "Sit back and relax. Let me get dinner ready for us then after that we can take a dip in the pool… and you know what comes next, baby." Rio stood in front of Bonita and thrust his pelvic area.

"Boy!" Bonita swung, but Rio jumped back to prevent being hit. They shared a laugh.

CHAPTER 9

Bonita and Rio enjoyed a romantic meal consisting of Benihana's steak, shrimp, lobster tails and chicken fried rice. Then they played around in the pool like kids for over an hour, both sliding down the slide from the loft area and splashing in the pool below.

After noticing Bonita yawn for the third time in a row, Rio suggested they get ready for bed by taking a bath in the Jacuzzi. He was running the water while Bonita searched through her luggage for pajamas she knew she wouldn't need. Settling on a pink thong and tank top, Bonita closed her luggage and grabbed some Japanese Cherry Blossom bath gel from the side pocket.

"Damn! That shit smells good!" Rio exclaimed, inhaling deeply to get another whiff as Bonita continued to squeeze it under the running water.

"Damn!" Bonita's eyes got wide as saucers as she mimicked the classic Chris Tucker face from *Friday*. "You must stay hard!"

Rio had removed his swimming trunks and was standing behind Bonita butt ass naked. His dick was rock hard and had a slight curve to the right.

"All this is just for you." Rio was slowly stroking his humongous dick with a cocky smirk on his face. He pulled at the strings on Bonita's bikini, causing the bottom to fall to the floor. Rio poked his dick through the gap between Bonita's legs and cupped her breast, while using his mouth to tug on the strings holding her top on.

Feeling Rio's thick, hard dick grinding against her pussy lips caused Bonita to lose control. Dropping the bath gel, she grabbed Rio's dick and began to jack him off while still rolling and twisting her hips against his hardness between her legs. Her back was against his chiseled chest and he was pinching her nipples, causing her to buck and moan even more.

"Come here." Rio pulled Bonita down to the cold marble platform surrounding the tub then pulled her ass to the edge while kneeling between her legs.

"Ohhhhhhh... ohh... ohhhhh," Bonita moaned as Rio began to lick her like a lollipop.

She tilted her head back and watched through the mirrors surrounding the tub as Rio sucked, slurped, buzzed, and hummed all up in her pussy. *Okay, it's official... Rio is the headmaster! Damn! This shit is the truth! Don't catch feelings, Bonita,* she thought while enjoying the way Rio was making her body melt.

"Oooooooohhhhhhh shit!!!!!!" she yelled out in ecstasy. *No this nigga ain't eating my ass and my pussy at the same time!!! How the hell he doing that shit?! Do not catch feeling for this nigga,* she thought as she adjusted her position so she had a better view of Rio. "Uuuuuuuugggggggggg... uuggggg... ooohhhh... uuuggggg." Bonita's body stiffened as she had an explosive orgasm, shooting cum all over Rio's nose.

Rio wiped his face with his hand then rubbed it on his leg before turning off the water. "Sit on my lap." He sat on the edge of the tub with his feet in the warm fragranced water.

Bonita stepped down into the tub and carefully positioned her throbbing pussy over Rio's python. Giving herself time to adjust to his size, she slowly lowered herself until she was able to pick up a good rhythm. She gripped the edges of the tub to steady herself then changed her stroke. Rio's reflection in the mirrors let her know he was enjoying every minute of it.

"Oohh shit! I'm 'bout to cum… turn around." Rio lifted Bonita and attempted to turn her facing him.

Bonita hesitated. "Wait a minute. I might fall and bust my head in the tub."

"Just put your feet around my waist. I'ma hold you. You not gon' fall."

Holding on to Rio's shoulders, Bonita turned around and put one of her legs around his waist. She hesitated before moving her other leg. "I might fall when we get to fucking, Rio."

"Baby, you can trust me," Rio said, grabbing her leg and assisting her with straddling him.

Now face to face, Rio lifted Bonita up and guided her on his dick. She hadn't sat in the tub yet, but she was already dripping wet. This allowed her to slide down on his rod with ease.

"Feel good… don't it?" asked Rio, smirking at the look of satisfaction plastered all over Bonita's face as he palmed her ass and lifted her up and down on his dick.

She opened her eyes before responding. "Just don't drop me, nigga."

Rio laughed before a serious look took over his face. "You can trust me, Bonita. You can trust me," he said, not missing a stroke.

Bonita looked deep into Rio's eyes, way beyond the surface, and at that moment she felt like she really could trust him. She began to buck even harder, meeting each of Rio's thrust with one of her own. Her long, wet hair swung from side to side as she lost all inhibitions and totally put her trust in someone for the first time since Krystal had died.

Moments later, Bonita had the most mind blowing orgasm she ever experienced in her life. The feeling was so intense she was almost sure she had pissed and shitted on herself. Rio had cum at the same time and slid down in the tub so he could release Bonita safely and rest his now rubbery arms. After turning on the jets, Bonita lay in Rio's arms and let the warm water and Rio's gentle touch make her forget about her life back home.

𝕯

"Dinner tonight... and every night from now on," Rio reminded Bonita of the promise she made during their two day stay at Sybaris. The time away did just want he was hoping it would do. He felt like he broke through with Bonita and was looking forward to spending more time with her.

Bonita kissed him on the lips then dug her keys out her purse. "Okay. Like you said... I gotta eat every day. I'll make sure we at least meet up for dinner. Grab my bag."

Rio and Bonita jumped out the truck and walked around to the back to get the bag. Just as Bonita pushed the button to pop the trunk on her rental, shots exploded, many of them hitting Rio's truck as both he and Bonita ducked for cover.

Bo rolled under her car, retrieving the baby Eagle 9mm from her purse in a swift motion. As she searched the area to figure out where the shots were coming from, she spotted Rio similarly positioned under his truck brandishing a dessert eagle.

Where the hell that gun come from? This nigga been packing all this time? They both thought about the other.

Bo spotted a figure dressed in all black with a weapon drawn creeping through the cars in the parking lot. She held eye contact with Rio for a split second then diverted her eyes in the direction of the shooter. Once he was clearly in view, Bo let off three shots, catching the shooter in the leg and collarbone.

Rio slid from under the truck and threw Bonita's bag in the opened trunk. "Get out of here!" he shouted, slamming the trunk shut.

Bo was already getting in the car and quickly backing out. As she approached the back exit she heard shots being fired. The faint sound of the Southfield Police's sirens could be heard. Bo spun out in traffic, nearly side swiping a man in a silver Chrysler Town and Country. *Welcome back from paradise*, she thought as she maneuvered her way to the freeway.

Bo's ringing cell phone broke her from her thoughts. She exhaled deeply once she saw it was Rio calling. "Are you all right?"

"Yeah... I'm straight. My bad back there. I don't know why the fuck somebody was shooting at me. For real... you gotta believe me," Rio pleaded his case. The thought that Bonita was the intended target of the shooter never once crossed his mind.

"I'm just glad we're both all right. We need to get off these phones though. I'll see you later." Bo watched a lot of crime shows and was paranoid about being linked to a crime based on cell phone records.

"Wait! What was up with you bangin' gats and shit? What—"

"Okay, see you later," Bo cut him off. She hung up the phone and tossed it over in the passenger seat. *At least he thinks somebody was shooting at him. Just like a nigga... think a bitch ain't got no business. Now what the fuck I'm gon' say I had a gun for? I'll think of something*, she thought as she made her way home.

𝔇

"Bonita, I really need to see you as soon as possible. It's imperative..." Chris repetitively spit into the phone.

Bonita had just taken a relaxing shower and lay down to take a nap before seeing her next client. Chris had been saying the same thing for the last fifteen minutes and she had heard just about enough. "Look, Chris. I told you I've been out of town, and I have to catch up on my work. I'll call you when I can see you. Good bye!"

She cut the phone off before sitting it on the nightstand and laying down for a much needed nap. Her time away with Rio had left her physically and mentally exhausted. At this point, she welcomed any dream... even the nightmares she had been having at least four days a week.

Ringgggg... ringgggg... ringgggg!

"What the fuck!" Bonita shouted. The shrill sound of the business phone ringing had startled her.

She jumped out the bed and ran over to the dresser to search through her junky purse for the phone. The phone was equipped with a device that changed Bonita's voice so the caller on the other end heard what sounded more like Barry White than a female's voice.

"Hello," she said, finally finding the phone.

"Bo... this Chip... I was... ummm... calling to... ummm... you know... check on that... check on that... ummm... job."

Would this mutha fucka just spit it out! Bo thought. It was starting to look like she wasn't going to get that nap.

"Did you... ummm... get the... get the... ummm... money?"

Chip was anxious to get rid of the forth member of his crew. They had successfully robbed the Motor City casino for five million dollars. The agreement made between himself, Greg, Jason and Merco was to lay low and not spend any of the money. That was three weeks ago, and

Merco was already being spotted on Seven Mile in a brand new 2008 Maybach 57S. *This stupid ass nigga ridin' 'round the D in a fuckin' $400,000 car! He gots to go! This nigga is not gon' get me caught,* Chip thought.

"Yeah, every thing is all set for today," Bo replied. She stretched out her arms and yawned deeply.

Chip let loose a sigh of relief. "Oh... okay... that's what's up, man. Ummm... just to let you know... he don't be at his crib that much no more. I heard the nigga got a room... up in Greektown Casino."

"Okay... it'll be done by daybreak."

Bo turned off the phone and sat it next to her other one. She had to get some rest before getting at Merco later on that night. She was hoping she would be able to catch him at his house, now she would have to find him then get him alone.

𝔇

Getting Merco would prove to be more difficult than Bo anticipated. She easily got his attention in the casino, but she couldn't chance killing him in his room, because she was sure the cameras would capture her entering and leaving. He was so full of himself he refused to leave the casino with her. Finally, after wasting hours trying to convince Merco to leave with her, she decided to call and have Chip lure him out of the casino by telling him to meet him at his house. Now she was following behind the Maybach headed to Merco's house.

Merco had Bo follow him to his house because he was paranoid and didn't trust a mutha fucka. He figured if Chip was on some bullshit the girl would at least be a distraction. He didn't care that the girl would know where he lived at. He knew this would be the last time he ever set foot in his house, because he planned to get everything he wanted out when he left after meeting with Chip and never return.

"Hey! Don't block me in!" Merco yelled as Bo pulled in the driveway behind him.

"Oh, my bad," replied Bo as she backed out the driveway and parked in front of the house.

Merco cautiously looked around as he rushed to put his key in the lock and open the door. He grabbed his gun from his waist as he entered the dark house. "Come on," he said to Bo.

Bo hesitated upon seeing Merco draw his weapon. "Maybe this is not a good time for you." She attempted to turn around and head back to her car.

"Bitch, get yo' ass up in here. I got too much money to be bullshitting out here. I'm just being cautious. I just gotta meet my boy right quick… then we out this bitch and back to the casino."

"Okay." Bo hesitantly walked in the house, gripping her purse tightly.

"Have a seat," Merco said to Bo before walking off to continue searching the house. Once he was satisfied they were alone, he placed his gun on the coffee table and sat down next to Bo on the couch.

Bo was anxious to get this over with so she could meet up with Rio for dinner. She had already wasted hours trying to get Merco out the casino. "Can I go to the bathroom?" she asked sweetly.

"I need to go with you. Damn, you fine as hell. Come here," Merco replied, licking his lips lustfully.

Bo leaned over closer to Merco. He forcefully grabbed the back of her head and began to tongue kiss her. Slob covered her mouth and chin and a foul smell filled her nostrils as he sloppily kissed her. When he finally released her, she couldn't wait to get out of there so she could wash her mouth off.

After getting directions, Bo hurried off to the bathroom and immediately used her hands to splash hot water on the lower half of her face, trying her best to scrub the foul smell away. Next she washed her mouth out with hot water. She had never smelled anything so funky in her life. *This mutha fucka never been to a dentist in his fuckin' life!* Bo thought. She could still smell his funky breath on her face.

Upon exiting the bathroom and entering the living room, Bo noticed a large black duffel bag on the chair that wasn't there when they first came in the house. She knew what was in the bag and was even more anxious to get this job over with.

"We up out this bitch, lil' mama... soon as we get to the hotel I'ma fuck the shit outta you," Merco smiled, showing his cruddy, crooked teeth. "Let me run this bag to the car right quick. I'll be right back." Merco reached for the duffle bag.

"Wait a minute, Merco. I can't let you do that."

"You what?" Merco spun around to find Bo standing with her gun drawn.

"Ya boy Chip sent me to holla at you for him. You flossin' a little too hard, Merco. Chip thinks you gon' get them all knocked... so he sent me to take care of you." Bo's eyes never left Merco's.

"Wait a fuckin' minute! Bitch, I'ma kill—"

One shot to the head stopped Merco in his tracks. His body slid to the floor as if in slow motion. Bo walked over to him and put another one in his forehead before grabbing the heavy bag and rushing outside to her car. She struggled to get the bag to the car, but finally did. She didn't bother searching the house, because she knew all the money he had was already in the bag or at the room in the casino.

Bo headed over to Union Street to meet Rio for dinner. She thought about taking the bag to the house first, but decided to put it in the trunk once she got to the restaurant. She tried to call Rio to tell him she was running a little late, but she kept getting his voicemail. Bo was excited about what could possibly be inside the large duffel bag. She was hoping this would be enough for her to stop killing and start living. She was seriously thinking about letting Rio into her life full-time.

Bo pulled in the parking lot on the side of the restaurant. She popped the trunk then exited the car, throwing the bag in the trunk before walking over to pay the three dollar fee to the parking lot attendant. Bo glanced around the lot looking for Rio's car. She caught herself worrying about him as she entered the restaurant and waited to be seated.

"How many tonight?" the young hostess asked. She was dressed in black tights with a striped red and black skirt, white blouse and black combat boots. Her pale skin was an apricot complexion and she had jet black hair and finger nails.

"Two please… smoking if you have it," Bo responded, glancing around the restaurant, once again looking for Rio.

The hostess led Bo over to a table across from the bar then placed two menus on the table before walking away. A few moments later a short black man came over to the table.

"Hello. I'm Chuck and I'll be your waiter today. Can I get you something to drink while you wait on your other party?"

"Sure, get me a shot of Remy on the rocks. Make it a double… oh, and could you please grab me a pack of Newports out the cigarette machine?" Bo grabbed a ten dollar bill out her purse and handed it to him. "You can keep the change."

"No problem. I'll be right back."

Bo tried to call Rio again and again she got no answer. After two double shots of Remy and five cigarettes, Rio walked into the restaurant smiling from ear to ear. Bo stared at him from head to toe. She noticed smeared blood stains near the bottom of his jeans and red speckles of blood on his white Air Force Ones.

"Where the hell you been? I've been calling you for hours," Bonita complained.

"Just give me a hug, baby." Rio pulled Bonita's chair out so she could stand to give him a hug.

Bonita noticed Rio hugged her extra tight. He kissed her softly on the lips before releasing her and taking a seat on the opposite side of the table.

"Damn! You in here chain smoking. I didn't even know you smoked. What's up?" Rio wrinkled his brow in concern. He grabbed a cigarette from her pack and lit it up.

"I was worried about you, Rio. You're late. Then you come waltzing in here with blood on your pants and shoes. You tell me what's up." The intensity of Bonita's stare matched that of Rio's.

"I ran into some bullshit on the way here, but it's nothing I couldn't handle. I'm sorry I'm late… and I'm sorry you were worried about me. That's a good thing though." Rio smiled then winked at Bonita, dumping his ash in the ashtray.

"What you mean it's a good thing?" Bonita asked with confusion all over her face.

"That means you must care about a nigga… if you worrying that is." Rio smirked.

They ceased conversation to give the waiter their orders. Bonita noticed how evasive Rio was about the blood on his clothing. She made a mental note to ask him about it again later.

"So what we gon' do, Bonita. I can't have you worrying about me and shit." Rio chuckled.

"Very funny, Rio... you could have at least called and said you were gon' be late." Bonita pouted.

"Believe me, baby. I would have called if I could." Rio pulled his cell phone out his pocket and handed it to Bonita. "My battery is dead, baby. Look at it."

"I believe you, Rio. You don't have to show me your phone. You don't have to prove shit to me... it's not like you're my man or anything."

"What I gotta do to make that happen?" asked Rio. He grabbed the Long Island Iced Tea the waiter had just placed on the table in front of him and took a long swallow. "Who you fuckin' wit'... the lawyer guy?" Rio asked. "Who else?"

"I'm not fucking with anybody. Chris is just a friend. I'm single." Bo fumbled with the Newports before finally getting a cigarette out the pack and placing it between her lips.

Rio quickly lit the cigarette. "What's up with you and Q? Have you ever fucked him?"

Bonita thought before saying anything. She took a long pull from the Newport before answering. "No... I've never fucked Quincy."

"I think he still has a thing for you. He always liked you when we were kids. I remember when he first started working for yo' father. He had to be around twelve... thirteen years old. He told me yo' father said he was gon' groom him to be his right-hand man and one day he wanted him to be his son-in-law. That nigga really took that shit seriously." Rio laughed.

"Yeah... my father did think of Q as his son. I always had a thing for you though, Rio," Bonita boldly stated.

"Oh yeah... tell me about that." Rio took a sip of his drink then pulled on the Newport, tilting his head to blow the smoke up.

"I like you a lot, Rio. I really do..."

"Why does it sound like I hear a 'but' coming?" Rio asked.

"Because you do," Bonita laughed before continuing. "I do like you, Rio, but I'm scared. I'm scared to get close to you... or anybody for that matter. Every time I get close to someone... they die. Sometimes I think I was meant to be alone. Like maybe I'm being punished and I don't deserve to be loved." Bo held her head down. She was wondering if she'd said too much.

"Being punished for what, Bonita? You haven't done anything wrong. It's not yo' fault what happened to yo' parents... and it's not yo' fault what happened to Krystal. Life is just fucked up like that sometimes."

Bo thought about what Rio had just said then quickly changed the subject. "Who the hell was shooting at you?"

"I don't know," Rio answered honestly.

The waiter sat their meals on the table. "Can I get you anything else," he asked. Hearing no, he quickly walked away.

"Just relax, enjoy your food, and let me take care of you tonight, Bonita. Is that cool?"

"Yeah, that's cool," Bonita answered, shoveling a spoonful of mashed potatoes in her mouth. She fully intended on letting Rio take care of her tonight.

During the meal, they both thought about the night they had endured. Each of them harbored secrets they were sure would scare the other off if ever revealed. Bo was hoping tonight would be the start of a brand new life for her. Rio hoped the same thing for himself. The two had more in common than they could ever imagine.

After dinner, Rio and Bonita headed to the Atheneum Suite Hotel where they checked into a deluxe suite for the night. As soon as they entered the room, Rio ran a hot bath for Bonita. He could tell she had some heavy things on her mind and wanted to help her relax.

After bathing her, he gently dried Bonita off then slipped his T-shirt over her head and led her over to the bed. Rio pulled back the covers. "Get in the bed."

Bonita did so with no resistance. Her body felt as if it was about to shut down. "Where you going?" she asked when Rio turned to walk out the room.

"I need to make a few calls then I'ma take a shower. I'll be back in a minute. Get some sleep."

"Okay." Bonita turned over in the big, comfortable bed and shut her eyes tight. Moments later, she could faintly hear Rio talking on the phone.

"All three of them niggas dead, man... don't worry about it. I got you, cuz. I'm at the room now... I'll holla at you tomorrow."

Bonita heard Rio turn the shower on before she fell into a deep sleep. When she woke up, Rio was easing in the bed behind her in only his boxers. He kissed her neck as he snuggled up against her and held her tightly while they both dozed off to sleep.

CHAPTER 10

Bonita listened as the newscaster spoke about Detroit continuing to claim the number one spot as the murder capital of the world year after year. She went on to say that 70% of the murders committed in the city of Detroit are never solved. A twinge of guilt ran through Bonita as she realized she was helping Detroit obtain this status by adding to Detroit's murder rate on a daily basis. She avoided watching the news for this reason.

After getting over a half million dollars from Merco, Bo began to decline hits. She now had close to two million dollars stacked and was ready to begin phase two of her plan to escape the Murda Mitten. Only two things stopped her from packing up her computer and leaving Detroit for good. One was the fact that she still hadn't chosen a place to move to and the other was Rio. As much as she hated to admit it, Bo was in love with Rio.

Bo knew it was time to go. She knew she was pressing her luck by staying in Detroit and chancing running into Stephanie or any of the other loved ones of the people she had murdered in cold blood. She knew the smart thing to do was to pack up and leave right now. But Bo felt like the chance at having Rio in her life for good, having someone she could depend on, was worth the risk of something bad happening.

For the past two months Bo had managed to avoid dealing with both Chris and Q and was spending the majority of her time with Rio. Chris had called a few times, but each time Bo rushed off the phone with him, telling him she wasn't ready to talk to him yet. Q was another story. He refused to let Bo just blow him off. He'd been on her to do some hits for him and couldn't understand why she was so busy all of a sudden.

Bo turned down the news and answered her phone. "Hello."

"What up doe? I'm outside… open the door," Q said.

Bo instantly got irritated. "Why can't you call before you come, Q? I could have company in here. You so disrespectful," Bo complained.

"Just open the fuckin' door. I need to talk to you."

Bo hung up the phone and went downstairs to open the door. Q stood outside wearing jeans, brown Timberlands and a brown leather jacket. After opening the door, Bo waited for Q to enter then locked both locks.

"What was so important you had to come all the way over here instead of just calling, Q?"

"What's up with you and Rio?" Q asked bluntly.

"Why?" Bo responded.

"Are you fuckin' my cousin, Bo?"

"Why, Q. Why do you need to know what's up with me and Rio? What difference does it make?"

"You know how I feel about you, Bo. Are you fuckin' Rio?"

"I don't think that's any of your business, Q. You trippin'." Bo tried to walk away, but Q snatched her by the arm.

"You must be fuckin' him 'cause you ain't denying it!" Q hollered.

Bo snatched her arm back. "What the fuck is wrong with you, Quincy? Okay, I'm fucking Rio! Is that what you want to hear? I'm in love with him, Q. Rio is the only man I want to be with! Just be happy for us?"

"What! Be happy for you? I'm supposed to be with you, Bo. That was the fuckin' plan!"

"What plan?! What the fuck is you talking about, Q? Look... I'm done with all the hits... all that bull shit... I'm done. I'm about to leave Detroit, and I'm asking Rio to go with me. I'll always keep in touch with you, Q. You're the only family I have left." Bo reached out and touched Q's cheek gently.

Q jumped back as if he was appalled by Bo's touch. "What the fuck you even know about Rio? What... you think 'cause he used to spend the summers up here with us you know him? Y'all don't even really know each other! I know everything about you, Bo. Your father wanted me to take over his business and marry you when we got older. That was the plan. I was supposed to be with you."

"Look, Q. I can't help how I feel. I love Rio. You my brother... I'll always have love for you, but I'm in love with Rio." After seeing the hurt look on Q's face Bo added, "I'm sorry."

Q spun around quickly and headed for the door. "Fuck you, Bo!" he spat before slamming the door shut and rushing to get in his truck. Q's real rush was to get out of Bo's view before the tears he was struggling to hold in fell. It was out of his control. He had been in love with Bo for as long as he could remember. Q was willing to do anything to be with Bo.

Bo put on her shoes and grabbed her jacket and purse before heading out to her car. She decided to drive the Mercedes to see how it was riding since it had just got out the shop from having the AK bullet holes repaired. As soon as she got in the car she put in Anthony Hamilton's CD and turned to "Since I Seen't You," putting it on repeat. The bass from the music vibrated the speakers in the luxury vehicle.

With no destination in mind on the cool fall day, Bo ended up on Seven Mile. As she drove around aimlessly, she thought about her parents, Krystal, Quincy and Rio.

She thought about all the people she had killed over the last twenty months and all the people those deaths affected. Bo smiled as she thought back to a memory of her father and Q not long before her parents were murdered.

"Quincy... come on in here, son," Bo's father Dale *yelled out to Q, who was outside messing with some girls from the neighborhood.*
"Here I come, pops!" Q got one quick smooch on one of the girl's butt before running in the house. "What up doe, pops?"
"What I tell you 'bout messing with those hot in the ass girls?"
"A hot in the ass girl will get a nigga killed," Q repeated as if he'd heard it a million times before.
"That's right. Those lil' bitches ain't good for nothin' but bustin' a quick nut up in... and ya betta make sure you force feedin' 'em them pills, 'cause they quick to pin a baby on a up and comin' nigga like ya self. I'm grooming you to take over this empire." He waved his arms in front of him. "I can't let my future son-in-law get caught up in no bull shit before he even gets all the way in the family." Dale laughed heartily.
"I ain't studin' them girls, pops. I was just playin' around." Q watched with fascination as Dale cooked up a half key of cocaine while simultaneously counting a duffel bag full of money.
"Okay... I'm jus' makin' sho... because my Bonita is a very special girl... and the man she's with won't have a bunch of bastard kids running around town. Bonita's like her mother. See... Janice is the type of woman that does it all. You understand what I'm sayin', Quincy?" Dale placed a large stack of money on the counter next to four other stacks similar in size.
"Oh... I know Bonita is way better than those other girls, pops. I can see that!" replied Q, his eyes focused on Dale as he stirred the cooking crack before grabbing another stack out the duffel bag and beginning to count while speaking.
"I ain't talkin' 'bout looks, boy! I'm talkin' 'bout having a bad ass bitch on yo' team. Janice will bust a cap in a nigga's ass if

necessary. Everything you see me doing… Janice can do it for me… if I ever need her to step in. Bonita's gon' be the same way," Dale said with a huge smile on his face.

Q's face took on a serious look. "You really think Bonita could kill somebody, pops?"

"You damn right!! Is my blood running through her veins? You damn right!! My girl is a thoroughbred! Bonita can and will do whatever it takes to survive. I taught her well!" Dale shouted. "If her mother had her way the girl wouldn't know shit about the game," Dale lowered his voice and said, "But I know how it is out here. I'm not gon' be here forever. Hell… some lil' nigga just like ya self may think he can take my place and try me one day. That's why I made sure Bonita knows how to shoot a gun and think for herself. I taught her how to separate her emotions from situations… like a man does. Don't ever underestimate a woman, Quincy."

"Alright, pops. I gotta go get this money from these niggas right quick. I'll bring it back tonight." Q grabbed a Faygo Rock & Rye out the refrigerator. "You think that's gon' be ready for me when I get back?" He pointed to the crack Dale was transferring to the blender. "I was gon' take everybody they sack tonight 'cause Bonita and Krystal want me to take them to the mall tomorrow."

"Yeah… it'll be ready. And tell them niggas to stop sittin' on the sack. I need this shit gone ASAP! I got a few keys of some good shit coming, and I want this bullshit gone when it gets here."

"Okay, pops. I'll handle it." Q shook Dale's hand before heading toward the front door.

Bonita sat on the stairs leading upstairs eavesdropping. She stood up as Q approached the door. "We wanna go to Somerset… not cheap ass Northland." Bonita turned around to head back upstairs to her room.

"Shut up! And stop ear hustlin' all the time." Q smacked her on the butt, but not hard enough to hurt her.

"You betta stop before I tell my daddy!" Bonita stomped off as Q walked out the door.

"Damn it!" Bonita pulled to the side of the road and grabbed her purse. She had been so deep in thought she didn't even know how long the officer in the unmarked car had been trying to pull her over. Fishing her license, registration, and proof of insurance out in record time, she rolled down the window and held them out to the approaching officer.

"We meet again," the officer said, ignoring the items in Bonita's hand and leaning down in the window. He was the same officer that got her out the club on that dreadful night downtown.

"Hello!" Bonita tried to play it off. "What happened to you that night?"

"Naw... you blew me off. You used me to get out of a ticket then to get out the club... and after all that... you still blew me off." The officer smiled.

"I'm sorry. I just got so caught up that night. I really did plan on going out with you. Maybe we could—"

"Maybe we can go grab a bite to eat right now. If you're not trying to get a ticket that is."

"I was actually on my way—" Bo tried desperately to get away from him once again, but he was persistent.

"Don't tell me I have to arrest you to spend a little time with you," he joked. "Just let me take you to dinner. I was on my way to meet my partner at Morton's, and I would love to gloat by showing up with you. Okay... he has a date and I don't. I said it. You look like you could care less about this."

"I'm sorry. I've just had a really long day and I'm really tired and I have some where I need to be."

"Wow! Three excuses in one! Am I really so bad that you won't even let me take you out for a nice dinner? Don't make me beg. I promise after dinner I'll never mess with you again if you don't want me to. I'll act like I never saw you before in my life."

"Okay!" Bonita surprised herself by saying. "I'll follow you."

"Thank you! Now if you try to lose me you know I'm going to chase you… right," he continued to joke.

Bonita didn't crack a smile. "I'm right behind you…"

"Ray… I remember your name, Bonita. Okay, follow me!" Ray took off to his car and sped around Bonita's car to lead her.

Bonita hesitantly followed behind Ray. "It could be worse," she said out loud. "At least we going to Morton's, so I know I'll get a good meal if nothing else. If I was a normal person I might even be interested in the nigga. He wasn't bad looking, but he wasn't Rio either!"

Bo parked next to a Chevy and got out the car. Ray quickly met up with her at the door of the restaurant. Bo looked him up and down as he approached. He was a dark-skinned brother with thick black eyebrows and long eyelashes. His faint mustache was barely noticeable unless you looked twice. His head held so many waves he had to have been brushing it at least twenty hours a day since he was five years old. He was about 6' 1" tall and had a solid, muscular build. For the first time Bonita noticed he was actually very attractive. But he didn't have shit on Rio.

Ray held the door open for Bonita to enter. As soon as she walked in the door she bumped right into Chris, who was accompanied by his receptionist.

"Um. Uh… Umm… Bonita. How are you? How have you been? I've been trying to get in touch with you," Chris stammered, his face was bright red. "I'm on a… a business meeting with my secretary here," he tried to explain.

"You don't owe me any explanation, Chris. Enjoy your night." Bonita attempted to step away from Chris.

"Bonita, wait!" Chris tried to grab Bonita's arm, but Ray stepped in and caught his arm in mid-air.

"Uh... Chris... I think it is. Bonita is here with me tonight, bro. So you gon' need to get at her on your own time," Ray said with bass in his voice.

Chris didn't even challenge Ray. He just gathered his jacket together at the collar and rushed out the door ahead of his pissed off date—the receptionist. Bonita was impressed by the way Ray handled the situation. She looked at him a little differently after that.

"Was that your ex or something?" Ray asked as they approached the hostess stand.

"No, just some one I used to date. With 'used to' being the key words." Bonita laughed.

"So I finally get a smile out of you," Ray joked. "I hope we run into a couple more guys you *used to* date if I'll get to see that pretty smile again."

Bonita smiled genuinely before looking in her purse for her cell phone. There was one text message. Bonita read the message and laughed out loud. The message read:

> *Bonita please come outside and talk to me. I'm not trying to get confrontational with your new boyfriend... but we have some unfinished business... Chris*

Bonita quickly texted back:

> *You a sucker ass nigga Chris! Lose my number nigga. Our business is finished!*

The hostess was leading Ray and Bonita to their table as Bonita was texting. Once they arrived at the table, Bonita put her phone back in her purse then took her jacket off. Ray pulled out her chair then sat down himself. Bonita finally looked up at the two people sitting on the other side of the table and her jaw dropped. With a sinister smirk on her face, there sat none other than Stephanie with the flirty cop, Ray's partner.

"So you did get a date," the flirty cop said to Ray. "I thought you were coming solo."

"Yeah… last minute change of plans," Ray replied, sliding in his seat and smiling at Bonita. "Bonita, this is my partner, Darryl. Um… Stephanie, right?"

"Yeah… I'm Stephanie… Bonita." Stephanie stared blatantly at Bonita.

"Darryl, Stephanie… this is my date, Bonita."

"I remember you," Darryl said. "You were supposed to call me. How you hook up with him?"

"Excuse me!" Stephanie said with an attitude.

"My bad… I'm just saying. I met her first," Darryl explained.

"We actually met her at the same time. I just happened to run into her again. And now… here we are. Can we just get some drinks or something?" Ray waved the waiter over. "Let us get… what would you like, Bonita?"

"I'll take a glass of Chateau Meyney," Bonita quickly replied. She needed a drink as fast as possible. *How the fuck is this happening. Of all the bitches in the world why the fuck is this bitch his date?* Bo thought as she looked around the restaurant, diverting her attention from Stephanie, who was still staring at her.

"I'll take a dirty martini and bring us a Prime Ocean Platter," Ray said.

"Anything for you?" the waiter asked Darryl and Stephanie.

"I'm good," Darryl responded.

Stephanie ignored the question. "Don't I know you from somewhere?" she asked Bonita.

"No," Bonita quickly replied. "You don't look familiar."

"Well, you sure do look familiar to me. Oh, I remember. I saw you at my boyfriend Tre's house... right before he got killed. Yep... that's where I remember you from." Stephanie picked up her drink and took a long gulp, her eyes never leaving Bonita.

"No... that wasn't me. I don't know anyone named Tre'. Maybe it was someone who looked like me," Bonita said innocently.

"This person drove a little silver Mercedes," Stephanie continued.

"Yep, that sounds like your car," Ray put his two cents in.

"I don't remember. I need to go to the restroom. I'll be right back." Bonita calmly got up from the table and made her way to the restroom.

Before she could gather her thoughts the door opened and in walked Stephanie. Bo instinctively grabbed for her weapon inside her purse.

"What, bitch... you think you can get away with killing me in the fuckin' bathroom? You got a lot of fuckin' nerves, bitch!"

"Yo' nigga shouldn't have been out robbing niggas and shit. He brought that shit on his self." Bo stood firm.

"Where the fuck is the money at? That was my money, too! I want my mutha fuckin' money!" Stephanie took a step forward toward Bo then thought better of it once she saw Bo's hand was still gripping her gun inside her purse.

"The money is gone. I can't do shit for you." Bo walked in a stall and locked the door.

"I've been asking around in the streets about females killing or robbing niggas. I was determined to kill the bitch responsible for Tre's death." Stephanie walked over to the mirror and began to mess with her hair. "I sat down and thought about what I did know. I knew you drove a silver Mercedes, but I wasn't sure which model. I knew you was some how associated with Q. You were close enough to him to be driving his Hummer. It wasn't much, but it was all I had."

"Q has nothing to do with this, Stephanie. Keep him out of it." Bo wiped herself then flushed the toilet. As she pulled her pants up Stephanie continued to talk.

"No matter what, I was hell bent on finding you and torturing you until you told me where the money was at. Time heals all wounds, Bonita… but I need that money back. If I don't get that money back—"

"Save your empty threats, girl. This was business. You shouldn't have been there. I'm trying to change my life. The money is gone. You get it… it's gone. I'm sorry about Tre', okay. I don't want to kill you, Stephanie…"

Stephanie turned and walked out the bathroom. *After I get back the money… that bitch is dead,* she thought as she walked back to the table. "I'm not feeling well, Darryl. You think we could do this another time?"

"Sure, baby. You got those drinks we already had, Ray?" Darryl was famous for skipping out on the bill.

"Go ahead, Darryl. I got you." Ray was just happy to finally have Bonita all to himself.

Bonita was in the restroom washing her hands and thinking of an excuse to get the hell out of there. More and more each day she was beginning to think it was time to just up and leave Detroit. She pulled out her cell phone and texted Rio.

We need to talk. Not now… I'll see you later – Bonita

Bonita was happy to see Ray sitting alone when she got back to the table. Ray seemed even happier than she was.

"They had to leave. I'm so glad to have you all to myself," he admitted.

Bonita smiled. "Actually, I feel the same way, Ray. I just wasn't in the mood for the catty female bullshit. You know what I mean?"

"Yeah... Stephanie can be a bit much at times. Darryl's only been dating her for about two months. Actually, they met the night we pulled you over. They met outside that club."

"Oh, really... that's interesting." Bonita picked up her glass of wine and swirled it around expertly before deeply inhaling it. She took a small sip and let it sit on her tongue, savoring the fruity flavors. Satisfied with the quality of the wine, Bonita took a full sip then placed her glass back on the table.

"You're really into wine, huh?"

"Just something my dad taught me. Actually, I was only twelve when he taught me how to taste wine," Bonita said with a faraway look in her eyes as if she was reminiscing.

"Twelve! Are you serious?"

"Yeah... my parents died when I was fifteen. They were murdered at our house."

"I'm so sorry. Bonita... are you an only child?"

"Yeah, but I had a best friend named Krystal... I called her Krys for short. She was murdered too. She died one week after her twenty-first birthday." Bonita shook her head from side to side as if to clear the thought from her mind. "I don't know why I'm telling you all this." She took a long sip from her glass of wine.

"You can tell me anything... it'll stay here at this table with us. It looks like you need to get some things off your chest. We all have skeletons from our past... let's leave them here at this table tonight." Ray grabbed Bonita's hand and gave it a gentle squeeze. "Do you think your parents and Krystal's murder were some way connected?"

"No. I think my parents were murdered in an attempted robbery. I don't know why Krys was murdered. It just doesn't make sense."

"What happened?" Ray asked with genuine concern.

"I really don't know. We had recently moved into our own place. Everything was going good for us. One day," Bonita paused to sip from her glass. "The day before Krys was murdered she was acting really strange. We talked about everything… there were no secrets between us since grade school. But for some strange reason I feel like she was holding something in. I questioned her about it… asked her what was on her mind. I knew her like I know myself… so I knew something was wrong."

"What did she say," Ray interjected.

Bonita paused, her head shifted slightly to the right and her eyes looked as if she was deep in thought. "She said it was nothing… but she was standing there with tears falling from her eyes. She went to bed early that day and the next day when I woke up she was already gone. I found out her body was found in an alley in Detroit the next day."

"And they never found out what happened to her… I remember that case." Ray sounded as if he was surprised.

"Nope… I guess nobody cared. To them she was just another black girl from the hood that probably wasn't doing anything with her life anyway. Things like that are not even shocking when you from Detroit."

"No… that case was really bothering the detectives working it. If I remember correctly… the victim was strangled. The body was wrapped in a blanket… but her head was also covered with a pillow case." Ray noticed Bonita's demeanor visibly change. "I'm sorry… let's talk about something else."

"Ray, why does life have to be so difficult?" Bonita looked Ray in the eyes and asked.

"I really do believe life is what you make it, Bonita. I grew up in the hood. Dexter and Linwood area... but I still managed to do something positive with my life," Ray said proudly. He went on to tell Bonita all about his life and how he got to where he was at today.

"Life is what you make it, huh?" Bonita lowered her eyes and tucked in her bottom lip as if deep in thought. "Excuse me for a minute, Ray." Bonita left the table and headed to the restroom. After making sure she was alone, she pulled out her phone and called Rio.

"What's up?" Rio answered. "Hustlaz Ambition" by Young Jeezy played loudly in the background.

"Hey... I think I'm ready to leave Detroit. Um... you coming with me?"

"Right now?" Rio lowered the music in his truck. He took a long pull from the blunt of Kush he was smoking then took a quick swig of Hennessy from the blue plastic cup resting in the cup holder.

"I mean... not literally right now, but as soon as possible. I just want to get out of here. Q confronted me about us today."

"What! What he say?"

"He stopped by my place and asked me if we were fucking around. At first I didn't say anything and he got pissed."

"Oh... Q knows where yo' house is at but you don't trust me enough to let me come to yo' house?"

"Rio, this has nothing to do with that. I want us to move together. I want to be with you. I'll text you the address. You can come to the house whenever you want to. Just say you'll leave with me."

Rio smiled. He hit the blunt hard, coughing for a few seconds before responding in a raspy voice. "Where we going, baby?"

"I'll text you my address. Meet me at my house tonight. We can decide where we wanna go and when we leaving then."

"Okay." Rio finished his drink then poured another from the pint that sat on the passenger seat, all while puffing the blunt and driving with his knees.

"Bye." Bonita hung up then texted her address to Rio. She felt good about the positive changes she was about to make in her life. She fixed her hair and put on a fresh coat of lip gloss then went back out to the table.

"Is everything all right?" Ray asked, concern wrinkling his brow.

"Yeah… everything is great." Bo relaxed in her seat as the waiter approached with their appetizer. She could tell Ray was an all right guy and debated on keeping in touch with him when she left Detroit for good.

CHAPTER 11

For the past two months as fall turned into winter, Bonita and Ray kept in touch by phone at least three days a week. Ray was quickly breaking down her walls and becoming a friend. He was a great listener and very easy to talk to. Sometimes it even slipped Bonita's mind that he was a police officer.

That night at the restaurant with Ray was a break through moment for Bonita. It was the day she decided to open her heart and allow someone to love her and actually reciprocate that love. After eating, Bonita and Ray sat and talked for hours about their childhoods, teenage years, and eventually their lives as adults. For the first time since losing Krystal, Bonita revealed things about herself to someone. She even told Ray about her feelings for Rio and how his cousin was in love with her and was hatin' on their relationship—without naming names of course.

Now as Bonita put the finishing touches on her make-up, while waiting on Rio to call and say he was on his way, she talked to Ray on the phone.

"Whose wedding are you going to again?" asked Ray. He was just getting in from working a double and began undressing as he used his shoulder to hold his cell phone up to his ear.

"One of my boyfriend's boys… some guy he said he grew up with. It's supposed to be a really big wedding." Bonita grabbed her 9mm and unscrewed the silencer then wiped everything down and placed it in her oversized bag.

"Have a good time... you'll probably catch the bouquet." Ray, now dressed only in his boxers, placed his department issued weapon on the nightstand then lay in bed.

"I don't know if I'm ready for all that." Bonita put on the gloves that matched her pant suit, grabbed her coat and headed downstairs. "That's him calling now, Ray. I'll talk to you tomorrow," Bonita said, looking at the caller ID.

"Okay, have a good time." Ray hung up the phone then placed it on the nightstand next to his gun before turning on to his side and closing his eyes.

Bonita clicked over to the other line. "Hey... change of plans." She grabbed her keys and headed out the door.

"What's up? You not selling me out are you?" Rio asked.

"Of course not... I'm just gon' have to meet you there." For the first time since her first hit, Bonita could feel the nervous energy bubbling inside her stomach. She'd been having second thoughts about going through with this hit for months. When Rio asked her to go to his boy's wedding with him and it just happened to be the same wedding she had confirmed to do a hit at over a year ago, once again she thought about backing out. But she never ended up calling to cancel. So here she was, headed to a wedding with her boyfriend, intending to kill the groom.

"Okay, baby. You know where the hall is at, right?"

"Yeah, right there on Southfield... the weird shaped building on the right."

"Yep... call me when you get there." Rio was focused as he made a U-turn and headed back toward the wedding.

"A Woman's Worth" by Alicia Keys played softly when Bonita started the car. As she backed out the garage she thought about the phone call she got on Thanksgiving Day last year.

"Hello. Is this Bo?" a deep male voice resonated through the phone line.

"Yeah... what's up?" Bo's altered and equally deep voice responded.

"I need you to handle something for me. I heard you were the person to call." There was a brief pause before he added, "My daughter's boyfriend just proposed. She intends on getting married in December of next year."

"Okay. When you want this done by?"

"That's the thing... I'm sure he'll fuck up and the wedding will probably be off by this time next year. But if for some reason he does manage to manipulate my daughter into marrying him... then I want this done on the day of the wedding... at the wedding. I'll pay extra if necessary," he added as if an afterthought.

"I'll need to be paid for this as soon as possible... $20,000 cash. If for some reason my services are not necessary... for any reason... there is no refunds."

"I understand. How do I get the money to you?"

"I'll have someone pick the money up for me tomorrow at one o'clock. You will go to the Outback restaurant on Middlebelt in Livonia... sit in the last booth on the left in the bar area. Have the money in a brown paper bag. Order lunch, eat and when you leave at exactly one o'clock... leave the money on the seat facing the door. You got it?"

"Yeah... I got it. I'll be there... uh... thanks," he awkwardly said.

Bo looked at the sparkles in the fresh white snow as she drove toward the Southfield Freeway heading to the wedding. *I hope this is the last time I do this. I'm really pressing my luck with this shit. Just three more months and me and Rio out this bitch!* Bonita thought as she drove. *I bet Ray wouldn't think I was such a sweet person if he knew what I did to make money.*

No one... no one... no onneeee... can get in the way of what I'm feeling...

Bonita grabbed her phone and looked at the caller ID. "Fuck he want!" she said out loud, answering the phone reluctantly.

"Bonita... thanks for picking up this time. I really need to talk to you. I miss you... I just want back what we had before. I'm so in love with you, Bonita," Chris groveled into the phone.

"You can't be serious, Chris. Why are you still calling me? I don't want to see you anymore." Bonita swerved to stay on Southfield and prevent merging onto I696, just missing a white Ford Taurus.

"Why? What did I do? I was having a business meeting with my receptionist... that was nothing."

"Chris, it has nothing to do with that. Look... I'm in a relationship. It's serious. Please respect that and quit calling me." Seeing the building up ahead, Bonita got over to the right and turned into the parking lot. "I gotta go, Chris."

"Is it Q? Or that guy I saw you at Morton's with? What—"

"Chris... none of that matters... we are over. Goodbye." Bo hung up the phone and threw it in her purse. She reached for the handle to open the door.

No one... no one... no onnnnnneeee... can get in the way of what I'm feeling... No one... no one... no onnnnnneeee... can get in the way of what I feel for youuuu...

Bo fumbled around in the oversized bag looking for her cell phone. Finally finding it, she quickly answered. "Hello."

"Bo... I need to talk to you... it's important." Q's voice was emotionless.

"Are you all right, Q?" Bo had not spoken to Q since she'd confessed her love for Rio to him. She was hoping he'd finally come around and was ready to accept her and Rio as a couple.

"I'm good. I need to talk to you in person. Can you meet me somewhere?" Q sat in his dark house in baggy jeans and a black wife beater. He hadn't bathed in days and was drinking out of his sixth bottle of 1738 in the past four days.

"I can… but not right now. I'm kinda out right now. Can I call you when I leave here?" Bo saw Rio pull up and rushed to end the call.

"Yeah… just call me when you leave there. As a matter of fact, won't you just come over my house when you get free?" Q looked around at the nasty house, contemplating telling her to just meet him somewhere.

"Okay. I'll call when I'm on my way." Bonita paused before adding. "I really missed you, Q. See you later." She ended the call without hearing Q's response.

Rio approached Bo's door just as she was hanging up the phone. She quickly closed her disheveled purse, concealing the gun from Rio's sight, then put her phone in the outside pocket after cutting it on vibrate. Rio opened the door and held out his hand to help Bonita out the car.

"You look good," he complimented her, shutting the door.

"Thanks… so do you." Bonita gave Rio the once over and approved of what she saw. Although she thought he was a little casual for a wedding, in slacks and Gucci loafers.

"Let's get inside. It's cold as hell out here." Rio held Bonita's hand as they made their way into the venue.

As they approached the usher standing at the door leading to where the ceremony would take place, he held out programs for both of them. "Are you a guest of the bride or the groom," he asked.

"The bride," Rio responded.

The usher led them to the benches on the left side of the room. As soon as they sat down, Rio jumped back up.

"I gotta go to the bathroom and see what's up with my people. I'll be right back."

"Okay." Bo looked around at all the guest present for the big event. Black and white roses filled the stage and huge bouquets were placed at the end of each row of benches. The combination of colors was strange to Bo and caused her to think of the irony of it all. *Black and white roses... white for weddings... black for funerals.*

Bo waited for Rio to exit the doors leading out into the lobby area before fleeing her seat. She'd visited this venue acting as if she was scouting a location for her wedding, so she knew the layout already. Rushing into the bathroom, Bo went in a stall and pulled out her gun. She screwed the silencer on quickly then stuck it in her waistband, closing her coat to conceal the weapon. Just as she was about to exit the stall, she heard someone entering the restroom.

"I still don't believe she's about to marry that trifling mutha' fucka" a high-pitched voice said.

"He's just using her for her father's money. That nigga fucked the stripper at his bachelor party. I know for a fact 'cause she's my baby daddy's cousin. He already got four kids by four baby mommas," a second voice added.

"Girl... I wouldn't even be in this wedding if everything wasn't paid for. And she gave us all that expensive ass jewelry as a bridal party gift. Shiiittt... I wasn't passing that shit up!" high-pitched exclaimed. "On the low... I know that's my cousin and shit, but I fucked that nigga right before he proposed to her ass at Thanksgiving dinner!"

"Girl... you lying!"

"I'm not! That nigga do got a big ass dick. That's probably why he got her ass brain washed."

Bo exited the stall, startling both of them.

"Damn! I ain't know somebody was in here!" high-pitched said loudly.

The other girl looked like she was about to shit her panties. Both girls wore black and white bridesmaid dresses with diamond jewelry accessories.

Bo ignored her, exiting the bathroom and heading for the groom's dressing room in the back of the building.

"Everyone needs to get in their places! The wedding is starting in less than five minutes! Where the hell is the groom and best man?!" The frazzled wedding planner scurried around with a clipboard in her hand yelling. As she headed in the direction of the groom's dressing room, she noticed the two bridesmaids exiting the restroom. "Ladies! You are supposed to be lining up at the entry! Get in your places now!" She turned around abruptly and ushered the girls toward the entry.

Bo casually eased her way toward the rooms in the back of the building. As she walked down the long hallway, she thought back to the day she took a tour of the building and recalled which room the tour guide told her was the groom's dressing quarters. Satisfied she was entering the correct room, Bo slowly pushed the handle to open the door and walked inside, letting the door close behind her.

Upon entering the room, Bo gasped at the sight before her. Both the groom and his best man lay sprawled out across the floor—dead. There wasn't much blood from what Bo could see. The best man appeared to have two small gunshot wounds to the chest and one to the side of the head, where a small pool of crimson red blood began to form. The groom lay in an awkward position with his head propped up against the wall. He had one shot to the forehead. A thin line of blood cascaded down the bridge of his nose between his still opened eyes.

Bo scanned the room before quickly heading back to the door. Slowly, she opened the door and peeked out. Seeing no one in the hall, but hearing the wedding planner's loud, irritating voice heading that way, she quickly dipped out in the hallway and headed out the side exit. She ran to the left of the building and all the way around to where her car was parked. By the time she got her key in the ignition, people were starting to exit the building in a mad rush.

A quick right and Bo blended right in with the heavy traffic on Southfield Road. Before she could get to I696 her cell phone rang.

"Hello," Bo answered with a nervous tinge in her voice.

"Where are you?!" Rio shouted into the phone.

"I'm on the freeway. Everybody started leaving and I didn't know what was going on... so I just left," Bo lied with ease.

"Pull over. Where are you? Meet me at the National Coney Island on Gratiot." Rio wondered what was up with Bonita. He'd come back to his seat to find her gone.

"Okay. I'll be there in a few minutes—"

"Just wait for me," Rio cut her off before hanging up.

"What the fuck is going on?" Bo said out loud as she reached speeds up to 90 mph and quickly exited at Gratiot. The Coney Island was to the left, so she put on her signal light and turned on Gratiot, entering the parking lot in no time.

Bo looked around the parking lot before removing the gun from her waist. She screwed the silencer off and placed in it her glove compartment, making sure to lock it afterwards. Bo placed the gun in her purse and grabbed her lip gloss out. Her mind was spinning about what had just happened back at the wedding as she put gloss on her lips.

A truck that looked like Rio's caught her attention and caused her to throw the gloss back in her bag and watch the truck as it made a right on Gratiot and a left to enter the parking lot. The truck pulled in the spot next to Bo and the driver looked over and smiled at her. It was Rio.

They exited their vehicles at the same time. Rio rushed over and embraced Bonita tightly. "I'm so happy you're all right! Somebody got shot at the wedding! I was so worried about you!" Rio said between kisses on Bonita's cheeks and forehead.

"What! What happened?" Bo played it off as they entered the restaurant. She really was curious to know what the fuck had happened. What ever the case, the job was done and there were no refunds under any circumstances. Bo wanted as much money as possible to start her new life with Rio in three months when they planned to relocate. They were still debating on the exact location, but Bo really didn't care where they went, as long as it was far away from Detroit and all the demons that haunted her there daily.

They sat at a booth and both ordered immediately before resuming their conversation. Bonita put cream and sugar in a steaming hot cup of coffee before asking, "Where were you?"

"I went to see what was up with my boy and he was getting ready... you know... putting the finishing touches on his hook-up. I told him I'd see him at the reception and gave him some dap then headed back to my seat. When I got there... you were gone. Where were you at?" Rio looked over at Bonita inquisitively.

Bo took a sip of her coffee then said, "I was in the bathroom."

Rio looked at her as if he wasn't convinced she was telling the whole truth, but said nothing. He downed a glass of water and called the waitress over to refill his glass.

"So who supposedly got shot?" Bo asked once she realized Rio wasn't going to respond.

"They said the groom and his boy." Rio took a huge gulp of water then placed the straw in his mouth and began to chew it.

"Your boy?! That's horrible. Bo caught herself getting loud and lowered her voice. What the fuck happened? Who shoots up a wedding?"

"I don't know what the fuck happened. I just saw everybody running and saying ole' boy got shot, so I headed for my car and took off. I was worried about you." Rio grabbed a lock of Bonita's hair and twirled it around his fingers.

"I didn't know what was going on. I was scared," Bo reached out and grabbed Rio's hand, gently holding it in hers.

"I'm sorry baby. I got you at some ghetto ass wedding where niggas getting killed and shit. Can we get a room up the street when we leave here? I wanna work all that tenseness outta yo' neck." Rio reached across the table and roughly massaged Bonita's neck, running his fingers through her hair in the process.

"I can't wait to leave here," Bo said softly, sipping her coffee again.

"Where we going, baby? We gotta choose a place." Rio sat up straight and took the straw out his mouth. He ran his fingers through the parts in his braids then placed the straw back in his mouth. "What about Cali?"

"I don't know if I wanna live in Cali. The freeways are fucked up, paparazzi is everywhere fucking with people all day, the property is expensive as hell," Bonita went on to say everything she hated about California. "What about Atlanta? We could get a nice house in Atlanta for way less than we would spend in Cali," she rationalized.

"Hell naw! Every nigga I know got a crib in Atlanta or somewhere in Georgia. I thought we was trying to get away from these same muthafuckas we see everyday."

"We are... okay... what about Colorado?"

"All those fuckin' mountains and snow... you jokin' right?"

The waitress placed their food on the table then quickly left. She returned moments later to refill Bo's coffee and Rio's water. "Can I get you anything else right now?"

"Naw... we straight," Rio responded with a mouth full of Hani Special. "Hey... let me get a Heineken," he called the waitress back to the table. "You want a glass of wine or something?"

"Yeah... I'll take a glass of Merlot," Bonita replied.

"We gotta figure out where the hell we going," Rio stated as the waitress returned with their drinks.

"Okay... what about... ummm... how about we move to... Tampa or Orlando... maybe even Jacksonville."

Rio looked as if he was about to protest but Bonita continued before he could.

"We would have nice weather and be away from the hurricanes. We wouldn't bump into people from here like we might in say... Miami. I think Florida would be a great place for us to raise kids."

"Kids! Oh... we having babies now," Rio teased.

Bonita blushed in embarrassment. She was shocked at how open she was with Rio. "You know what I mean... it's a nice place to live."

"I don't know... I kinda wanna go west. What about Vegas... naw... my beggin' ass cousins live there. Hey... I got it... Arizona? Not a hot ass part of Arizona where niggas rolling in town every week to pick up a bundle, a chill part of Arizona. With nice houses and good schools and shit," Rio said with a wink.

"Arizona sounds good. I think I might like it there." Bo imagined living in Arizona. She had never been there, so her first thought was of the bad ass house Angela Bassett had in the movie *Waiting to Exhale*. "Yeah... I think Arizona might be the place." A smile spread across Bonita's face as she stuck a fork full of chili & cheese fries in her mouth.

"Yeah... when niggas start getting killed at they wedding it's definitely time to move the fuck on," Rio joked. "So now that we decided on Arizona, we gotta come up with a city in Arizona."

"I don't know nothing about Arizona. I'm gonna have to research that on the internet. We still have a few months before we leave," Bo reminded him.

"You gon' be ready?" Rio asked, raising his eyebrow.

"Hell yeah I'll be ready. I'm ready now." Bo grabbed Rio's hand to get his full attention. "All I need is you and I'm good, Rio. You believe me when I say that... don't you?" she asked in a serious tone.

"Yeah... I know that, girl. I been waiting on this for a long ass time... so you know I'm ready." Rio demolished his food then threw his napkin on his plate. He picked up his beer and drank it in one gulp.

"Damn! Slow down." Bonita laughed.

"I'm trying to get up in that." Rio reached under the table and rubbed Bonita's crotch.

"Get the check," Bonita said between bites.

Rio paid the check and the two left the restaurant with Bonita following Rio to the nearest hotel.

CHAPTER 12

"Bonita! What the hell is you doin', girl?!"
Bo had been lost in the moment, rolling her hips as she bounced on the dick. She quickly rolled over in shock, grabbing the sheets to cover her naked body. Her hair was wild and strewn all over the place. She held a small knife in her right hand while gripping the sheets close to her chest with the other.
Just as shocked as Bo, Q sat up and covered his privates with his hands as best he could. They both stared at the intruder in silence for a few seconds then Q jumped up and ran out the room, balls swinging as he gripped his dick to hide it from view.
"What the fuck is y'all doin'?!" the intruder asked again.
"Krys, what the fuck you bustin' up in here like that for?" Bo threw the knife across the room, just barely missing Krystal's head as she ducked to the left to prevent being hit.
"Bitch, is you crazy?!" Krystal ran over to the bed, diving on top of Bonita and holding her down. "What the fuck is you and Q doing fucking? You shouldn't be fucking him! You shouldn't be fucking him, Bo!!!" Krystal began wildly swinging at Bonita, punching her in the head with both fists.

Bo awoke to the sound of her business phone ringing. In the typical greedy nature of humans, she had decided to continue to stack paper while waiting out the last few months before she would disappear to a Scottsdale, Arizona suburb with Rio. Bo took a moment to get her head together before answering the phone. The dream she'd just woke up from seemed so real.
"Yeah," Bo answered.

"I need your help," a soft-spoken woman replied. She paused before continuing. "My five-year-old daughter was molested." Her voice cracked as she began to sniffle. "The monster responsible for doing this to my baby... his case was dismissed because the evidence was tampered with. Please tell me you can help me."

Pangs of sympathy flooded Bo's heart. Still shook and confused by the dream, she didn't respond for a moment.

"Are you still there?" the woman asked.

"Umm... yeah... I'm here. Tell me everything you know about this person."

"How much is this going to cost me?" the woman asked. She'd been told by the person who referred her to Bo that the man charged $10,000. That was all she had to her name. Ironically, it was in the savings account she had opened for her child's education when she found out she was pregnant. But she was willing to spend every penny of it to make sure that monster would never hurt her child, or anyone else's child, again in this lifetime.

Bo thought for a moment. She could feel the pain in the woman's voice through the phone. She imagined a grown ass man forcing himself on a five-year-old and it infuriated her. "One thousand... we'll discuss how you'll get the payment to me later. Tell me where I can find this... guy at." *I'm going to enjoy this shit*, Bo thought. *I'm going to make this mutha fucka feel just as bad as he made that little girl feel.*

𝕭

"Glad you finally made it," Q said sarcastically as he moved to the side to allow Bo entry.

"I'm sorry, Q. You know how this shit keeps me tied up." Bo entered and immediately noticed how nasty the house was. "You need to get one of yo' bitches over here to clean this shit up," she joked. Her plan was to look around his room for Krystal's diary while she was there.

"What's keepin' you so tied up? You told me you wasn't doing shit no mo'." Q subconsciously began to pick up trash and dirty dishes, placing it in the garbage and sink.

"I'm still working, Q. I changed my mind. I'm going to stick to the original plan and do the damn thang... until it's time for me to get up out of here." Bo began to help Q straighten up.

"Why you ain't tell me? I been sending all my work to... to this other nigga. You missed out on some major money." Q walked in the dining room and began cleaning off the table.

Bo had begun washing the dirty dishes. "It's cool. I've been pretty busy anyway."

"What you working on now," Q yelled so Bo could hear him over the running water. Passing Bo in the kitchen, he walked in the living room and turned on the sound system then cut the TV off before going back in the kitchen.

"I got this one nigga who raped a five-year-old I gotta handle. Then there are the twins and the insurance hit. That's all I got for the rest of the week." Bo bounced her head to the Blade Icewood song Q had put on. "Boss up and get this money," she sang along with the song.

"Damn! A nigga tryna fuck a five-year-old. That's some sick shit. You need to torture that nigga." Q went back in the dining room and grabbed the last of the dirty dishes from the table, putting them in the soapy dish water.

Bo thought about telling Q her plans to move to Arizona, but she decided to wait. The vibe she felt between the two of them was slightly different. And although she couldn't quite call exactly what was wrong, she knew something was different between them.

"Thanks for helping me get this place together. You know I can't function without you." Q stepped behind Bo while she continued to wash the dishes. He moved her hair behind her right ear and softly kissed her on the cheek. "I'm glad we cool again," Q whispered softly in Bo's ear.

Bo slightly jumped at the feel of Q all up on her. "What was you mad at me about anyway, Q?" she questioned, already knowing the answer.

"Let's finish this then we can talk about everything." Q retreated to the living room where he began cleaning up.

Ding! Dong! Ding! Dong!

"You expecting somebody?" Bo asked. The doorbell surprised them both.

"Hell naw!" Q made his way to the side door and looked out the window. *Fuck this nigga poppin' up over here fo'*, Q thought as he opened the door for Rio.

"What up, cuz?" Rio stepped inside the house all smiles.

Bo could smell his *Unforgivable* by Sean Jean before he made it up the stairs and into the kitchen. She smiled upon seeing Rio. He sported a brown Sean Jean wool jacket with indigo Sean Jean jeans and brown Timberlands. A brown and tan skully covered his freshly braided hair.

"What up? What you doin' over here washing dishes?" Rio asked Bonita as he stood where Q had been just seconds before. He kissed her softly on her left cheek.

"I just stopped by to kick it with Q, and the house was a mess... so we just started cleaning it up. You would get here when we're almost done." Bo turned around and snuck a quick kiss on Rio's lips. It amazed her how right it felt when Rio stood behind her and how wrong it felt when Q stood in the same spot.

"Shiiit... I ain't tryna clean this nigga's shit no way!" Rio laughed. "Let me holla at you right quick, dawg," he turned to Q and said.

Rio and Q headed down to the basement, leaving Bonita to finish the dishes. As soon as they hit the bottom step, Bonita was in Quincy's room searching for the diary. She looked through all the drawers and in the closet then looked under the pillows on the bed and under the couch cushions. Feeling like it was taking her too long, she gave up her search and headed back in the kitchen in the nick of time. Moments later they both came back up to the kitchen.

"Let's go grab something to eat," Rio said, resuming his position behind Bonita.

"We still got shit to talk about," Q interjected.

"All, man that shit can wait… she'll call you when we finish eating," Rio said.

"Yeah… I'll just give you a call later," Bonita added, drying her hands and grabbing her coat.

Q was visibly pissed off. He said nothing… just stood there with his lips tight. His body tensed up as Bonita hugged him before walking out the door with Rio behind her. "Ain't that a bitch," Q said to himself, slamming the door and locking it.

"You wanna leave yo' car here and ride with me?" Rio asked.

"Yeah, just let me park on the street though," Bonita replied, rushing to get over to the driver's side of the car. In her rush, she slipped on an ice patch and lost her footing, causing her to fly up in the air then fall hard on her ass.

"You okay?" Rio asked between laughter. "Damn… you bust yo' ass!" He continued laughing as he ran over to help her up.

Bo lightly chuckled, obviously embarrassed. She glanced up and could have sworn she saw Q looking out the window cracking up. "I'm straight." She brushed herself off then carefully walked over to the other side of the car.

After parking on the street, Bonita got in the truck with Rio and they drove off.

"What you got a taste for?" Rio asked.

"Um... I don't care." Bonita still couldn't believe she fell.

"What about some Max and Erma's?" Rio adjusted the volume on the radio so he could hear her.

"That's cool." Bo rummaged through her purse to answer her ringing work phone. "Hello."

"Yeah... I got a job for you," a female's voice said.

"Okay... you know how this goes?"

"Yeah... I leave the ten stacks wherever you say and once you get the money and info on the mark you'll handle it... right?"

"Yeah... pretty much. What's the name and reason?" Bo asked. She glanced over at Rio to see if he was paying attention to her. He wasn't... he was searching through the CDs on the side of his door.

"The bitch name is Bonita. I don't have a lot of info on her, but I can tell you the address her car is registered at. This bitch killed my man and now she gotta go! I tried to get at the bitch myself, but her and the nigga she was with both start busting at me and my boy. They got my nigga."

Bo's jaw dropped at the realization that the hit was being put on her. *This gotta be Stephanie's bitch ass*, she thought. "What's that address?"

"You all right?" Rio asked, noticing how upset Bonita was beginning to look.

She nodded her head up and down, indicating she was fine. Bonita tried to hide her shock as the caller said her home address. "Okay... call me tomorrow at noon for the place." Bonita looked over and smiled at Rio, trying to ease his concern.

"Okay... I want this bitch gone by the end of the week. Is that possible?"

"It should be... we'll talk tomorrow." Bo ended the call and turned the phone off.

"You sure you okay?"

"Yeah." Bonita grabbed Rio's free hand. "I'm fine... just hungry." Rio had put in Boney James' CD, *Ride*. Bonita closed her eyes and bounced her head to the beat of the first song, "Heaven". "And I'm embarrassed, too," she added.

"It wasn't that bad," Rio lied, unable to hold in his laughter.

Bonita punched him in the arm. "Quit laughing at me!"

🆅

Dinner turned into a night at the Courtyard on Orchard Lake and Twelve Mile. Bonita woke up the follow morning butt naked in Rio's arms. They had sexed all night long until they were both sweaty and exhausted before passing out.

"You finally up," Rio said, morning breath kicking.

"How long you been up?"

"About an hour... I was just watching you sleep. You looked like you was sleeping well."

"Only when you're in bed with me," Bonita admitted.

"We only got a couple more months and we outta here... right?"

"You still don't believe me?" asked Bonita.

"I'm jus' saying. We would leave now if it was up to me." Rio adjusted his arm which had fallen asleep under Bonita's weight.

"A few more weeks and we out... it's gonna go by so quick. This last month flew by. Just think... Christmas is next week."

"I know... let's go somewhere," Rio suggested. His eyes sparkled in excitement.

"Go where?"

"Umm... what about Paris... or Amsterdam!" Rio sat up.

"I can't go overseas. I don't even have a passport, boy!" Bonita laughed.

"What! You need to get a passport. What if we need to flee the country? Yo' ass would be stuck here. We can go somewhere else. Hey... let's go back to Sybaris!"

Bo thought about what Rio had said. "I got some stuff to do over the holidays. I really can't go out of town." She got up and began getting dressed.

"What you doin'! Come back over here!" Rio protested.

"I really need to get back to my car. I got a lot of stuff to do today." Bo looked in her purse, which she had buried under all her clothes, to make sure nothing looked disturbed. She was a light sleeper, so she was sure she would have felt if Rio got out the bed.

"What you gotta do?" Rio asked. He hadn't moved at all.

"I gotta... umm. I got that—" Bo stammered.

"You don't gotta do shit! Is you cheating on me?" Rio asked jokingly.

"Hell no! Rio, I don't want you to think that." Bo rushed back over to Rio's side. "I'm not messing with anyone but you. We're leaving here in March, Rio... seriously." She looked him in the eyes as she spoke.

"I'm jus' fuckin' with you... but I did want some more pussy before I started my day."

"If you don't get up... it's not like you won't see me tonight!"

"You want me to stop by the house tonight?" Rio asked, finally getting up and beginning to get dressed.

"No," Bo said quickly, realizing Stephanie had her home address. "Why don't we just meet back here?"

"Okay. Let's grab some breakfast and I'll take you back to yo' car." Rio put the last of his clothes on.

"Can I get a rain check on the breakfast? I have an appointment in an hour... I forgot about it," Bo lied as they left the room. All she was thinking about was grabbing her computer and a few necessities and getting a room somewhere she could lay low for the next few months.

Bo gave Rio a quick peck on the lips when he pulled up next to her car. "I'll call you a little later, okay?"

"Yep," Rio replied, driving off once Bo had gotten inside her car and started it up.

Bo was waiting on the rear window to defrost before pulling off. She glanced to the right and saw Q looking out the living room window. "What the fuck is he doing up this early?" she questioned out loud. She thought about going to knock on the door but thought better of it.

As she drove off, Bo thought about the dream she had the other night. *I was fucking Q with a knife in my hand? And Krys was going crazy on my ass.* "Damn I miss you, Krys," Bo said. "I gotta get that diary before I leave. What the hell is Q doing with it anyway?" Bo continued to talk. "Damn, Krys... why you have to leave me? Q be trippin' sometimes... Rio, well... I'm really feeling Rio, but I'm scared. I hope he don't play me, Krys. Damn! I need your advice, Krys!"

Bo hit the steering wheel hard. She was beginning to feel like she was losing her mind. "Bust Your Windows" by Jazmine Sullivan came on the radio.

"Fuck it... I'm leaving right now! I'm getting the fuck out of here right now. This bitch got the nerve to put a fuckin' hit on me!" Bo continued to rant until she cautiously pulled into her garage, closing the door and putting one in the chamber before getting out the car.

After searching the entire house, Bo was comfortable she was alone. Immediately, she began to pack her computer and all her jewelry. After filling five suitcases with clothes, shoes and guns, she was ready to find a nice, secure, lo-key spot to chill at for the next couple of months.

CHAPTER 13

Christmas with Rio was Bo's best Christmas she could remember since her parents were killed. She didn't have to do anything, because Rio took care of dinner by ordering everything pre-cooked from the Honey Baked Ham store. He also made sure she had plenty gifts under the tree. They spent the day at Rio's place, where Bo had been staying since getting the hit put on her.

A week had passed since Bo successfully got the $10,000 from Stephanie, after which she promptly murked the bitch. She was sure Stephanie had tricked her information out of that sucka ass officer Darryl, and she was pissed off about it. As she lay in Rio's bed eating pistachios, watching TV, and talking to Ray for the past half hour, she thought about how she got Stephanie and ways to get back at Darryl's trick ass.

Bo sat crotched down in the damp, dark, decrypted building, waiting on Stephanie to make her entrance. She was careful to park several blocks away at the gas station on Greenfield and Fenkell and came over an hour earlier than she told Stephanie to come with the money. She positioned herself near a hole in the concrete that allowed her to view the side of the building, but could still clearly see the back entrance as well.

Stephanie pulled up alone in the old school Chevy. She looked around as she got out the car then grabbed the small duffle bag from the back seat. Bo watched as she walked a few feet to the alley then made her way through the back door. She pressed a button on her cell phone to use for light.

"Hello... is anybody here?" Before Stephanie could even realize her mistake, Bo appeared from the shadows of darkness brandishing a shiny, chrome Kel-Tec 9mm. *"I'm here with the money,"* Stephanie quickly said, not yet recognizing Bonita.

"Throw it over here and keep your hands where I can see 'em," Bo replied, disguising her voice the best she could.

Stephanie quickly complied, blinking her eyes as she tried to adjust them in the darkness. *"Look... I know you have to take precautions, but this is a little extreme. I'm just dropping off the money for this, damn!"*

Bo quickly grabbed the bag and rushed toward Stephanie. *"Bitch! Did you really think you were gon' put a hit on me and live? Did you?"* Bo fired a single shot into her stomach. *"You have to be the dumbest bitch in the D. What... you didn't know the infamous Bo and myself... Bonita... was one in the same?"*

Never actually hearing the shot, the realization of what was happening caused Stephanie to go into shock. Her eyes bucked, and she grabbed her stomach as if she was attempting to hold in the stream of blood cascading out. Doubled over and in disbelief, Stephanie looked up at the approaching figure and still couldn't believe her eyes. Her last thought was one of regret for not telling anyone her whereabouts. For obvious reasons, she'd kept the hit and her meeting to drop off the money to herself.

"You should have just left well enough alone... stupid, bitch." Bo fired two shots into Stephanie's head then quickly exited the building. She walked through the alley with her gun out for three short blocks then put it in her waistband as she approached the gas station. Bo hopped in her car unnoticed and merged into traffic on Greenfield headed toward I96.

"Yep... Darryl is crushed over that girl Stephanie getting murdered. I think he was really feeling her... 'cause he was with her every day he was off. Hey, are you trying to catch a movie or something today? You know I'm off for the next two days," Ray said. He brushed his hair then sprayed Hanae Mori on his shirt.

"Naw, I already got plans with my boyfriend. We can do lunch next week though. Hey… let me call you back later, Ray. I just thought about something I was supposed to do." Bo jumped out the bed, causing the bag of pistachios to fall to the floor where they scattered about.

"Okay… I'll call you tomorrow if I don't hear back from you today."

Bo ended the call then rushed in the guestroom, where she'd put all her luggage, to search for one of her silencers she'd been meaning to find. She'd only hung up a few items, so the majority of her things were still packed. Bo searched through each piece of luggage carefully, not wanting to disturb the order of her things, so she could tell if Rio had been snooping through them. She couldn't remember exactly where she hid the silencer and began to get frustrated after searching for several minutes and coming up empty handed.

"Where the hell did I put it at?" Bo questioned. She stopped searching to think for a moment. Bo smiled widely as it finally hit her. "I locked it in the glove compartment!"

She took off running to the side door then turned around and ran in the bedroom to grab her keys. Making it to the car in record time, she opened the passenger side door and unlocked the glove compartment. Bo paused before opening the glove compartment. She took a deep breath then opened it. Happy to see the missing silencer, she grabbed it and locked everything back up.

Bo headed back in the house. Just as she started to lock the door, she heard the loud bang of Rio's sound system as he pulled in the driveway behind her car. Not wanting Rio to know about the silencer, she looked around in a panic, searching for somewhere to stash it quickly.

Rio's keys were in the lock quicker than she anticipated, causing Bo to quickly open the cabinet and hide the silencer inside a large pot. She put a few smaller pots inside the larger one to conceal the silencer just as Rio entered the house.

"What's up?" Rio said as he entered then quickly rushed through the kitchen. "I gotta piss bad than a muthafucka!" he shouted.

Bo thought about moving the silencer while he was in the bathroom but changed her mind. She decided to just wait until Rio left the house before moving the silencer, not wanting to chance him seeing it.

Rio entered the kitchen seconds later, kissing Bonita on the lips before opening the refrigerator. He grabbed a can of pop, cracked it open and took a long swig before saying, "Why you not dressed yet?"

"Dressed for what, Rio? I'm chilling out today. I think I'm catching a cold or something. I feel sick." Bo was looking through the cabinets, not sure what she was looking for. She was prepared to stay in the kitchen until Rio left if she had to. Whatever it took to make sure he didn't find her silencer. "Did you even wash your hands?" She frowned up when she noticed his hands were bone dry.

Rio smirked. "Naw I ain't wash my hands. My dick clean." He finished off the pop then threw the can in the container reserved for empty bottles and cans. "Come here… let me feel your forehead." Rio reached over to touch Bonita, laughing as she jumped out of reach.

"Go wash your nasty ass hands!"

"Come here, baby." Rio rushed Bonita, grabbing her up and shuffling her toward the bedroom. "Daddy, gon' take care of you. What you need… some Vernors and soup?" Rio laughed as Bonita tried to squirm away from him.

"You so damn nasty! Stop!" Bonita shouted as Rio picked her up and attempted to place her in bed.

"What... this ain't yo' side?" Rio joked as he walked around to the other side of the bed. "What the fuck!" Rio plopped Bonita down on the bed then lifted his foot to inspect the bottom of his boot. "What the fuck is all this shit on the floor?" he asked, stooping down to get a closer look.

"Oh, I dropped some pistachios. I was gon' clean them up," she said nonchalantly.

"Why the fuck you ain't get them up when you dropped them? Talkin' 'bout I'm nasty. That's just trifflin'. You ain't keep yo' shit like that."

"Rio, I said I was gon' clean them up. Quit tripping. And I ain't trifflin'... you the nigga not washing yo' hands after you use the bathroom." Bo had gotten an instant attitude. She got off the bed and began picking the nuts up, tossing them in the small trash can sitting in the corner of the room.

"You shouldn't be eatin' in the bed no fuckin' way. Gettin' crumbs all in the bed and shit," Rio continued talking shit.

Bo ignored him and continued picking up the pistachios. Once she was finished, she grabbed her purse and went to the guestroom to get some clothes to put on. She looked up as Rio entered the room and stood, saying nothing.

"What you want?" Bo asked with an attitude.

"Don't get mad at me. You ate?" he asked.

"I'm 'bout to leave," Bo responded.

Rio walked over and bent down to hug her. "I'm sorry, baby. I'ma take you to pick up something to eat and we can get you some cough medicine while we out." Rio kissed her cheek then walked out the room.

Bo got dressed quickly and met Rio downstairs. She knew it was senseless to argue with him, because he more than likely had her car blocked in. As soon as they stepped out the house, Q pulled up.

"What up doe? Where y'all goin'?" Q asked, walking up the driveway.

"We 'bout to grab something to eat… what up, cuz?"

Bo looked at Q closely. Something just didn't look right with him. "What's up with you, Q?" she asked while opening the truck door.

"I need to holla at you right quick… 'bout some business." Q pulled his hat down even lower then looked up and down the street.

"Business?" Rio cut in. "What business you got with Q?"

Bo shrugged her shoulders and threw Q a menacing look. "I don't know! Ain't no telling what this nigga talking about."

"Let me holla at you right quick." Q began walking back to his truck.

"Let me see what this crazy ass nigga wants," Bo said, quickly following Q to his truck.

Rio watched as Q and Bo got inside the Hummer. He continued to stand outside and watch the two as they held a conversation.

"What the fuck is wrong with you?" Bo said as soon as she closed the door. "Don't ever come over here with that bullshit in front of Rio. He don't need to know shit about shit, Q. Don't be such a fuckin' hater."

"Whatever… I got a hit I need you to handle ASAP." Q fired up a Newport and blew the smoke in Bo's face.

Bo cracked the window to let the smoke out. "You couldn't have called my business phone for that? Don't come over here with that bullshit, Q. You hear what I'm saying?" Bo looked in his eyes.

Q laughed then took a long pull from the cigarette and blew out the smoke before saying, "This my cousin's crib. I coulda been coming for that nigga. You so worried about that nigga finding out you a killa… you need to be finding out who the fuck you sleeping with every night."

"I know who the fuck I'm sleeping with. Look, Q… just don't bring my business here. That's all I'm asking." Bo noticed Rio still standing outside the truck. He was looking dead at them as they talked. She rolled the window back up then said, "What do you need me to do, Q?"

"This nigga named Choc from the eastside. You heard of him?" Q rolled down the window and tossed the cigarette butt out then rolled it back up.

"I heard of him. You got any info on him for me?"

"Everything you need is in here." Q handed her a large envelope. "When can you have this done?"

Bo folded the envelope and stuffed it in her purse. She was trying her best to keep it on the down low. "Let me see what you gave me on him, and I'll call and let you know." Bo opened the door and jumped out the truck before Q could say anything. Before closing the door she said a little too loudly, "Boy, your birthday is months away. You could have called to ask me to plan your party. See you later." Bo shut the door and walked over to Rio's truck. "You ready, baby?"

Rio looked at Bonita with a puzzled expression on his face, as if he was in deep thought about something. He looked over at Q as he backed out the driveway then back at Bonita. "Yeah… I'm ready. What that nigga was talking about?"

"His birthday," Bo lied as they got in the truck. "He want me to put a party together for him."

"And he had to come all the way out here to tell you that? That nigga been acting a little off lately," Rio admitted.

"I know. I was just thinking that. I don't know what's wrong with him." As if on cue, Q's music began to bang as they pulled behind him at the stop sign on the corner.

"I know what's wrong with that nigga... he mad because he want yo' ass and you with me." Rio laughed. "He been acting like a little bitch lately. If that nigga wasn't fam... I wouldn't even fuck with him."

"Yeah... I'm feeling you on that," Bo agreed.

Rio turned the opposite way of Q and headed to the restaurant.

𝔇

A week passed and Bo was still a little under the weather, but she had to get this nigga Choc out the way. The information Q provided her with said Choc had to go because he talked too much. The place he hung out most was Skateland on Alter Road on the eastside. Now, as she stood facing the concession stand, girls mean mugged her as Choc continued to run his mouth.

"I knew you was from the Westside. I can tell when a broad is from the Westside. She just looks different. So what you got up after this? I'm tryna spend some money."

This nigga is just too damn stupid, Bo thought as she listened to him ramble on and on. Bo felt out of place and couldn't wait to get out of unfamiliar territory. As Choc ran his mouth, Bo looked around cautiously. She hadn't planned on having a long conversation with Choc. She really just wanted to catch him entering by himself and do him then, but as soon as he pulled up in his tricked out Grand Prix two females rushed to get out their car so they could walk in with him.

"Who you came here with?" Choc asked. Not giving Bo time to answer the question, he continued. "You trying to leave with me tonight?"

"You ready now?" replied Bo. She wanted this to be over with as soon as possible.

"Uh... yeah... but you can't come to my house. Where you stay at?"

"Where you park at? For what I'm trying to do we can just go out to your car."

"Damn! You out cold!" Choc was shocked by Bo's brazenness.

"What if somebody see us?" Choc couldn't hide his excitement. The idea of fucking the fine ass Westside bitch in his car, right in the Skateland parking lot, made it hard for him to control his emotions.

"You don't have tinted windows?" Bo played it off. She already knew his tints were past the legal limits.

"Yeah... I'm in that gold Grand Prix on twenties. I'ma go out first and you can come out in a few minutes. I don't need all these people in my business. I got you when you get out there." Choc quickly made his way to the exit, stopping once to tell his boy he would be right back.

Moments later, Bo went in a stall in the bathroom. She checked to make sure her gun was off safety and ready to go before screwing on the silencer and placing it back in her huge purse. She put on her black, dollar store gloves then made her way toward the exit.

Choc smiled as he saw the fine girl exit the building. She looked around the parking lot before spotting his car and walking over. He quickly popped the locks so she could enter. "I thought you changed yo' mind for a minute," Choc joked.

"Naw... I just had to freshen up a little," Bo replied as she entered the car and pushed back her hood.

"Oh, okay. So what's up?" Choc reached in his pocket, pulling out a knot. He peeled off two hundreds and handed them to Bo. "This is for your troubles... buy yourself something nice with it."

Bo laughed inside as she took the two bills and placed them in her purse. "Why don't you lay your seat all the way back and pull your pants down. You don't want shit all on yo' pants when you get back in there... do you?"

"Yeah... you right." Choc quickly complied, unfastening his belt and pants and pulling them down to his ankles. He hit the button on the side of his seat to let the seat fall all the way back.

It took everything in her not to laugh when Bo saw his three inch dick standing rock hard. "Oh, you trying to hurt somebody," she joked. "Before I do this... do you know a guy named Q?"

"Yeah, that nigga from the Westside... I know exactly who you talking about. He got a cousin named Rio from GR and the nigga drives a black Hummer with—"

Bo quickly came out her purse with her gun in hand, stopping Choc mid-sentence. "Yeah, he was right... you do talk too damn much," she said as she leaned as far away from Choc as possible before pulling the trigger, leaving Choc with his brains leaking in the back seat.

Bo waited a few minutes before exiting the car and walking over to her rental. She calmly got in the car and headed to I94. As she got on the freeway, she called Q.

"It's done" she said when he answered.

"You get anything? That nigga keep shit on him," Q said with excitement in his voice.

"I didn't even look. I had to get the fuck outta there. But he's done though." Bo couldn't wait to get to Rio's house so she could take a long bath and just relax. It seemed like every time she killed another person, a small part of her died as well. She couldn't wait for the next few weeks to pass so she could disappear with Rio.

"What! You coulda hit a lick. That nigga got money and bricks at his crib!"

"This my phone... not the business phone, nigga. It didn't work out like that. I'll holla at you later." Bo hung up. *That nigga, Q must be losing his fucking mind... talking reckless on my phone and shit. I can't wait to get the fuck up out of here for good.*

Bo's business phone rang, breaking her from her thoughts. "Hello."

"Now what the fuck happened? Why the fuck you ain't get that nigga then clean out the crib like I told you to?" Q yelled.

Bo couldn't believe he called her back for this shit. "Look, nigga. Getting him at his crib wasn't the best move for me. That nigga lived in the hood, and it's always somebody watching his house when he's not home. I wasn't about to chance doing it at his crib. I did what you paid me to do... anything extra is just that... extra."

"So you don't got shit for me?"

"Bye, Q." Bo hung up and tossed the phone in the passenger seat.

During the long ride to Rio's house, Bo thought long and hard about her life. She wasn't proud of what she'd become, but she rationalized by telling herself it was only temporary and would set her up for life. She wasn't sure exactly what Rio was bringing to the table financially, but she was going to do whatever it took to make sure they would be straight once they left Detroit.

Bo was happy to see Rio wasn't home when she pulled up. She rushed in the house to throw up. During the long ride to Grand Rapids she had begun feeling sick to her stomach. She wasn't sure if it was from the small piece of brain matter she'd noticed on the arm of her jacket, or the smell starting to permeate throughout the car. Either way, she was disgusted.

After throwing up, Bo took off her clothes, stripping naked, and left them on the bathroom floor. She grabbed a garbage bag from the kitchen then made her way back to the bathroom to put the items in it. Once everything was in the bag, Bo took it to the living room and tossed it in the fireplace. It was killing her to burn one of her favorite Gucci bags, but it had to be done. She grabbed the long lighter from the mantel then lit the logs the bag was sitting on top of. Bo stood and watched until the last of her clothing was burned and all that was left in the fireplace were ashes and the burning logs.

Bo made her way back to the bathroom to take a quick shower. For some strange reason she was drained and couldn't wait to lay down and go to sleep. During her shower she kept envisioning Choc's half blown-off face, which caused her to gag repeatedly.

After showering, she put on some comfortable sleepwear. As soon as her head hit the pillow she was knocked out.

CHAPTER 14

Bo agreed to meet Chris against her better judgment. He'd said it was imperative he speak with her, so she was curious to see what the hell he would have to say to her. Now, as she stood at the hostess stand at the Hard Rock Café in downtown Detroit, she regretted even bothering to come.

Bo was looking good in her tangerine Calvin Klein suit paired with brown leather shoe boots and a brown Al Wissam wool coat. She watched as Chris entered the restaurant wearing a long black wool coat with black leather shoes.

"Hello, Bonita. I hope I didn't keep you waiting long," Chris said as he walked over to Bonita and kissed her on the cheek.

"No, I just got here a few minutes ago myself," Bonita admitted.

"Table for two?" The hostess finally came over and asked.

"Yes... could you sit us somewhere we can have a little privacy?" Chris requested.

The hostess looked around the restaurant before nodding her head. "Umm ... sure... follow me," she said, leading them over to table in a corner of the restaurant.

Once they were seated, Chris wasted no time digging into Bonita. "It'll come as no surprise I want to talk to you about us. What happened to us, Bonita? I thought we were on our way to an exclusive relationship. I wanted to marry you one day." Wrinkles creased Chris' forehead as he stared at Bonita with sincerity in his eyes.

"That's not what I was looking for, Chris. I had a lot of fun with you. You're a great guy, Chris... just not the guy for me. I'm sure you'll find a great girl to settle down with."

"What! Are you serious! You had fun with me but I'm not your kind of guy? What kind of bullshit is that?" Chris asked, getting loud. A few of the other patrons looked over in their direction.

"Lower your voice, Chris. You're making a scene." Bonita looked around, obviously embarrassed.

Chris leaned in closer to Bonita, gritting his teeth. His face displayed a menacing scowl Bonita had never seen on him before. "I don't give a fuck about these people!" he said, lowering his voice. "I'm tired of being the nice guy and continuing to get played by bitches. If you weren't interested in me you should have never acted like you were. So what the fuck was I... just someone to pass time with? That's bullshit!" Chris' voice began to rise again.

Bonita stood up and began putting her coat back on. "I didn't come here for this shit, Chris. If you have something to say to me I suggest you say it right now, because I'm out of here."

"What!" Chris had lost it. "I don't even get the common courtesy of you listening to how I feel? You've got to be fucking kidding me!"

"Is everything all right?" the waitress finally appeared and asked.

Bonita grabbed her purse and headed toward the exit without saying a word. Chris quickly jumped up to follow her, leaving his coat behind. The waitress watched as they both exited the restaurant. Once they stepped outside, Chris grabbed Bonita's arm.

"What the fuck is your problem?" Bonita spun on her heels and yelled in Chris' face, snatching her arm away. "I never told you I was gon' be yo' woman, Chris! I never told you I loved you. Hell, I never even told you the pussy was yours!"

"Yeah... but you were fucking me like it was mine! Bonita, I'm in love with you," Chris' demeanor changed as he spoke. "I just want you to be mine. I love you."

Bonita began to laugh as she turned around and headed across the street to the black Chevy Tahoe she'd rented. "I'm done, Chris. Forget about me." Bonita stared at the truck parking two meters down from where she was parked. She shook her head as her suspicion was confirmed and Rio stepped out the truck.

"What the fuck you doing with that nigga?" Rio asked as he approached Bonita.

Bonita rolled her eyes when a smiling Q jumped out the passenger seat of Rio's truck and joined them. "He said he needed to talk to me about something so I met him here. Then the nigga started tripping so I left. It's nothing, Rio... really." Bonita looked back at the restaurant and saw Chris open the door and walk back inside.

"Why you ain't tell me you was meeting him then. I gotta roll up and catch you in some bullshit?" Rio wasn't sure what to believe. When Q spotted Bonita standing outside the restaurant with the man he referred to as Bonita's ex-boyfriend, he instantly said Bonita was probably creeping with the guy. This was causing Rio to second guess Bonita's loyalty to him.

Bonita stepped closer to Rio and hugged him. "I'm sorry, baby. I didn't want you to think nothing was up, because it's nothing. I love you, Rio," she said then glanced over at Q, who was frowned up.

"I love you too, baby, but you should be able to tell me anything. I thought we were here." Rio's fingers formed a peace sign as he pointed from his eyes to Bonita's.

"We are, Rio. I promise it won't happen again... okay?" Bonita squeezed Rio tighter.

"We'll talk when I get to the crib. You going home now?"

"In a few hours I'm heading back. I was planning on hitting up the mall while I was here. You know they don't have shit at the mall in Grand Rapids."

"Okay." Rio pulled out of her grasp. "I'll see you when I get home."

"Okay, baby." Bonita noticed the look of satisfaction on Q's face when Rio pulled away from her. "And, Q... don't be instigating shit."

"Shut the fuck up! You the one got caught out here with that lame ass nigga. I told you to hit that nigga a long time ago."

Bonita caught herself before gasping. She couldn't believe Q had said that. *This mutha fucka done lost his mind.* She looked at Rio but his expression hadn't changed. "I'll see you tonight," she said, kissing Rio's lips. Bonita hopped in the truck and pulled off quickly.

𝕯

Bo felt out of place at the crowded neighborhood bar with her suit on. She was deep in the hood on the Westside of Detroit. She thought back to the night she got the call for the hit.

"I wanna set up a hit," the young white boy said recklessly into the phone.

Although the business phone could never be traced back to Bo, she still hated when her clients didn't at least try to talk with finesse, under the circumstances. "You must have the wrong number," Bo responded, about to hang up.

"I forgot! I'll pay double!" the white boy screamed into the phone, catching Bo's attention and stopping her from hanging up.

"Twenty thousand and the necessary info need to be in a backpack under the table at Logan's on Ford Road in Canton. Sit in the bar area at the last table on your right. Eat something and leave the bag on the floor when you leave. Someone will be there to get the bag for me once you leave the restaurant. Understood?"

"Yeah, dude... I got it. My bad about earlier...."

Bo hung up the phone, not waiting to hear the rest of his apology.

Now as she sipped on her third apple martini, she tried to think of the best way to get her mark, a tall, dark-skinned guy named Roy who looked like a finer version of Busta Rhymes. She'd already sent him a drink, a double shot of Don Julio was what he requested, but he never came over to thank her or even acknowledge her. This took away a little of the guilt she was feeling over what she was about to do.

Bo pushed the skinny straw to the side and took a large gulp of her drink. Her mind drifted back to the day she got the money and the file on Roy.

Bo sat at the bar in Logan's and watched as the white boy entered restaurant and walked up the few stairs to the bar area. He went to his left then abruptly stopped, causing the waitress behind him to nearly drop the five mugs of drinks she was carrying.

"My bad," he said as he turned around and walked over to the last booth on the right, which just happened to be empty.

Bo watched as he ordered an appetizer and a draft beer then sat and ate before leaving as awkwardly as he'd entered. Once he'd left the restaurant, Bo stood from her stool.

"Can you have someone clean this table back here? I think I'm going to have something to eat and I'd like to sit there so I can see this TV," she said to the bartender, grabbing her half-filled glass of wine.

Bo quickly slid in the booth and grabbed the backpack off the floor. She took the money and folded up piece of paper out and transferred it to her purse just as the busboy came to clear the table.

"On second thought, I'm not really hungry," Bo said to the bartender as she walked over and placed a ten dollar bill on the bar to cover her wine and his tip.

"Okay, have a good day," the bartender said.

Bonita went in the bathroom and walked in a stall. She pulled the paper out her purse and began to read about Roy, the next man she would kill. The note said Roy was a thirty-five-year-old man that was having sex with a twenty-year-old girl, when he wasn't slapping her around. The girl was the white guy's sister. The note listed where Roy worked and all the bars he frequented and the days of the week he was usually there. Five nights a week Roy was out at somebody's bar getting his drink on.

Snapping back to reality, Bo watched as Roy stumbled over to the men's room. He tried the door, but apparently it was locked. Roy stumbled past the jukebox and down the hall to exit the back door leading into the alley.

Bo knew this was her best chance, so she got up slowly, trying not to draw attention to herself. She casually walked down the hall as if she was going to the women's room, which was also that way. Reaching in her bag, she grabbed the handle of her gun as she opened the back door.

Hearing the door open startled Roy, causing him to quickly turn around. His hand was wrapped around his thick dick as he continued to pee, just barely missing Bo's feet.

"What... you waaant some of thiiis?" he slurred, shaking his dick before stuffing it through the hole in his boxers and zipping his pants. He began to walk toward Bo.

Bo quickly pulled her gun out her purse. In her haste, she'd forgotten to put the silencer on. She glanced around to determine the quickest way to get to her car. Once she realized her error, it was too late.

Roy was drunk, but he moved swiftly, pouncing on Bo before she had a chance to let off a shot. He reached out and slapped Bo so hard, she flew into the brick building.

Bo's face was on fire and she'd banged her elbow when she hit the wall. She quickly regained her composure and fired two shots just as Roy ran over and reached for her neck. As Roy slumped to the ground, Bo fired an additional shot to his head then ran down the alley. Just as she got to the end of the alley, Bo fell hard. She quickly jumped up and ran down the street and around to the front of the building. Her panic slightly decreased as she spotted her car and made her way over to it.

Just as Bo was pulling off, people were starting to rush out the club. It had taken a few minutes for the club patrons to realize a shooting had occurred. The loud music camouflaged the sound of the gun shots, so Roy's body wasn't discovered until the next guy decided to take a piss in the alley.

Bo drove straight to Grand Rapids, hoping Rio wasn't home yet. She exhaled loudly after entering the house and realizing her prayers had been answered, she was home alone. She ran in the bathroom to look at her face. There was still a hand print on it.

"Fuck!" she said in frustration. Bo grabbed her phone and called Rio. "Hey, you on your way home?" she asked as if all was well.

"No, I'll be home in a few hours. I'm still in Detroit. You straight?" Rio thought Bonita sounded different for some reason.

"Yeah, I'm straight. I'll see you when you get home."

After ending the call with Rio, Bo ran a warm bath and soaked in the tub. While soaking, she decided that Roy would be her last hit. Enough was enough. *I just want to get the hell out of Detroit and start my new life with just Rio and I,* Bo thought before she began crying hysterically. "Only eight more weeks and we're out of here," she said out loud.

Bo got out the tub and wrapping a towel around her sore body. She had bruises on her elbow and her leg was bruised and scrapped up. Both her hands had cuts and scrapes from when she tried to break her fall. Tired and frustrated, she climbed in bed and dozed off.

"Bonita, wake up." Rio shook Bonita awake. "What happened to yo' face?" he asked.

"Huh?" Bonita grimaced in pain as she attempted to sit up. Her elbow and leg was still sore.

"What happened to yo' face? It looks like somebody slapped the shit outta you." Rio began undressing as he spoke.

"What time is it?"

Rio looked at his watch then took it off and sat it on the dresser. He removed his gun from his waist and sat it on the nightstand then let his pants fall to the floor. "It's three o'clock. What's up? What happened to yo' face?"

Bonita thought carefully before answering, "Ummm... I was... I was... I fell. I mean... I got into with somebody... that's how my face got that mark on it. But then I ended up falling later on and fucked my arm and my leg up."

Rio looked at Bonita like he didn't understand anything she'd just said. "What?"

Bonita eased from the bed. "I need to use the bathroom. I'm tired, Rio. I don't feel like talking about it." Bonita tried to walk out the room, but Rio blocked her exit.

"Which one is it, Bonita... the bathroom, you tired or you don't wanna talk about it? What's going on with you?" Rio held Bonita's face in his hands as he spoke to her, looking into her eyes.

"I'm just tired, Rio. I'm ready to leave here. I'm ready to leave now." Bonita began crying softly. "I'm in love with you, Rio. I don't want something to happen and we end up apart."

"Nothing is going to happen, Bonita." Rio paused before saying, "Are you still messing with that guy Chris? Just tell me the truth now." Rio looked deep into Bonita's eyes, hoping to detect if she was being honest or not.

"Rio, believe me... you have absolutely nothing to worry about with Chris. He means nothing to me... he never has meant anything to me. He called and said he had something important to tell me. I was curious to know what he had to tell me that he couldn't say on the phone, so I agreed to meet him at Hard Rock Café. That was it. I left before he could even tell me what he had to say, because he started talking like he was trying to get back with me," Bonita said sincerely.

"What about Q?"

"What about him?"

"Have you ever had feelings for him?"

"Never... I swear, Rio. Q has always been like a brother to me." Bo wanted to tell him about the one incident between her and Q, but she just couldn't.

"I believe you. Go pee and come get in the bed." Rio released Bonita then playfully slapped her on the butt. "Oh, and Bonita... I'm in love with you, too."

Bonita smiled as she made her way to the bathroom. *Whew! I got off easier than I thought I would. I still can't believe that nigga slapped the shit out of me. Yeah... I'm done with all that shit,* she thought.

CHAPTER 15

To Bonita's dismay, Rio pulled up in front of Q's house. Dealing with Q was the last thing Bonita wanted to do, on Valentine's Day of all days. Bonita never cared for Valentine's Day since this was around the time Krystal had been murdered. Q had managed to convince Rio to bring Bonita over his house after dinner for a nightcap with him and a friend. Bonita was not looking forward to spending time with Q or his date, who ever she was, but she agreed against her better judgment.

"We only gon' stay for a minute... alright?" Rio knew Bonita wasn't feeling it, but he'd promised Q he would stop by.

"Okay. One drink and I'm ready to go. Q's been tripping lately."

Q opened the door before they even exited the truck. "What up doe? Come on," he yelled.

"I guess we should get this over with," Bo said with an attitude.

"Don't be like that. One drink then I'ma take you home and blow ya back out." Rio laughed. I know that's what you really want for Valentine's Day."

"You damn right!" Bonita laughed with him.

Once they got in the house, Q led them to the living room where a short, brown-skinned girl sat on the loveseat. "Hi, I'm Kwana," she introduced herself.

"Kwana, this my cousin Rio and our girl Bonita," Q completed the introductions.

Rio and Bonita said hello and took a seat on the couch. Bonita noticed how Q introduced her as *our* girl and cringed. Each time she saw Q she was more and more irritated by him. The girl Kwana looked familiar, but Bonita couldn't place where she knew her from.

"What y'all drinking? I got Mo, Remy, beer and some 1800 Silver."

"You already know I'm fuckin' wit' the 1800, nigga." Rio jumped out his seat.

"I'll take 1800, too," Bonita responded.

"You sure you don't wanna sip some champagne? That's what Kwana drinking," Q stated.

"I want 1800," Bo responded dryly.

"Okay, I got you," Q said before heading in the dining room with Rio right behind him.

"You need anything to chase it with… pop, juice or a lemon?" Q yelled from the other room.

"Just make mine like yours, Rio!" Bonita shouted. A hit of an attitude came through in her tone.

"You look so familiar to me," Kwana said, trying to make small talk. "Did you go to McKenzie?"

"Yeah."

"I thought you looked familiar. I was Krystal's lab partner in biology. She used to tell me stories about how much fun y'all had hanging out on the weekends. Krystal was so cool. That's a damn shame they never found out who did that to her." Kwana shook her head.

"Did what?" Q asked as he and Rio entered the room with the drinks and bottle in hand.

"We were talking about them not catching the person who killed Krystal," Kwana said.

"Oh." Q's facial expression and disposition changed immediately when he thought about his sister. He sat the drinks down then walked to the back to his bedroom.

"You knew Krystal?" Rio asked.

"Yeah, we all went to school together. I recognized Bonita from McKenzie." Kwana took a sip of her drink then leaned back on the loveseat.

"I don't remember you?" Rio said, looking at Kwana.

"She didn't hang with Krys and me after school," Bonita explained.

"Let me go check on Q," Kwana said excusing herself.

Bonita downed her drink. She frowned up and cringed at the vile taste of the clear liquid. "How long we staying here? I'm ready to go."

"Okay, have another drink, and we'll leave in ten minutes." Rio kissed the top of Bo's head before refilling her glass.

Moments later, Q and Kwana returned to the living room. "You straight, Bonita," Q asked.

"I'm good. We're about to leave in a minute."

"Why y'all leaving so soon? Damn, y'all just got here." Q flopped on the loveseat next to Kwana. "What you need, Bonita? Just let me know and I got you." Q grabbed the bottle and filled his glass. He attempted to pour more into Bonita's glass but she quickly placed her hand over it.

"I'm straight. I'm not trying to get fucked up. It is Valentine's Day. I'm trying to get home," Bonita said then looked at Rio.

"Right... I feel you on that," Kwana said. "She trying to get home with her man, Q."

"This my fam, girl. Shut the fuck up," spit flew on Kwana's lip as Q said.

"Damn, Q." Kwana wiped her lip. "I'm jus' saying."

"We 'bout to be out, man. Let me go take care of my lady." Rio downed his drink then looked over at Bonita. "You ready?"

"Yep... just let me use the bathroom right quick." Bonita quickly downed her drink and headed down the hallway.

Bo could hear Q and Rio talking as she turned right instead of left and headed in Q's bedroom. She had been constantly thinking about Krystal's diary since seeing it that night. Bo went straight to the side of the bed and lifted the mattress. *I knew it!* Bo thought when she saw the purple diary laying under the mattress. She quickly grabbed it and stuffed it in her bag.

"Thanks for the drinks. Have a good night," Bo said when she entered the living room.

"Y'all some funny actin' mutha fuckas. That's all right though. Holla back." Q jumped up and headed to the door.

"Chill, nigga. I'll holla at you tomorrow. Handle yo' business." Rio nodded his head toward Kwana before walking out the door with Bonita right behind him.

"I'll talk to you later, Bonita. I need to holla at you about something," Q said, winking his left eye while snarling up his lip to the left and making a clicking sound.

Bonita turned around to look him in the eye. "I'm done, Q... don't even bother," she said through clinched teeth.

"I heard that before," Q said as Bonita got in the truck and closed the door.

"What that nigga Q talking about," Rio asked, turning down the volume of the radio.

"Q ain't talking about shit. I'm so ready to get the fuck out of Detroit."

"Yeah... I think I'm ready, too. What we gon' do when we first get there?" Rio looked over at Bonita.

"I guess we can get a room while we look for a house to buy. I have money put up, but of course we would have to just put a deposit down and pay a mortgage on the house. I was thinking about opening up some kind of business when we get there."

"Where you getting all this money, Bonita?"

"Huh?" Bonita turned her head to look out the window.

"You heard me. How you getting all this money you talking about? You be pulling disappearing acts and shit... I hope yo' ass not dancing," Rio said with a frown on his face.

"Hell naw... I'm not dancing." Bonita laughed. "You out yo' damn mind. You disappear a lot yourself... while you questioning me about my money. You know my father made sure I was okay."

"I'm just saying. I got my own money. You should trust me... we about to move to another state... just you and me... and you don't trust me."

"I do trust you, Rio. You're the only person I have in this world. Q... Q just been acting weird to me lately."

"Yeah... I feel you on that. He been saying some off the wall shit to me, too. That's my family though... so what can you do." Rio threw his hands in the air for a second.

Bonita sat and thought about the fact that Rio thought she didn't trust him. She was in love. Her thirty second rule was broken. She couldn't imagine living her life without Rio. She looked over at him and smiled. *Damn my baby fine. Can I tell him I been killing people for money? How you tell somebody some shit like that. He'll think I'm crazy as hell. He's selling drugs, but murder... I have to take this to the grave*, Bonita thought.

"What you thinking about?" Rio asked, interrupting her thoughts.

"Us."

"What about us?"

"I just don't want anything to happen. I love you, Rio, and I want you to trust me."

Rio remained silent.

"Look, Rio," Bonita began, "my father left me a lot of cash, and when I turned eighteen I collected on his insurance policy as well," Bonita lied with ease. "There was a time when I promised myself I wouldn't get close to anything I couldn't turn and walk away from in thirty seconds flat—"

"Ha, ha, ha, ha, ha... girl, you crazy as hell! That's that shit from *Heat*," Rio said, laughing.

"I'm serious, Rio!" Bonita yelled, mad he'd cut her off.

"Okay, I'm sorry, baby... go ahead." He continued to chuckle until Bonita looked at him with a frown on her face.

"I just want you to trust me like I trust you. Do you love me?"

"Yeah... I love you. I'm not fuckin' around on you, Bonita. I just be out in the streets handling business. I'm trying to stack paper for when we leave. I'm a man... I can't expect to live off yo' lil' money."

"I have over a million dollars at my house, Rio. We can use it to open up a business and live off. It's in the safe in my closet... it's a floor safe. The combination is my birthday. I love you, and I trust you." Bonita grabbed Rio's free hand and held it gently.

"A million dollars! Where the fuck you get all that money?" Rio had money, but he was far from a millionaire.

"I told you my dad looked out. I want to share everything I have with you."

"Damn... you trust me like that? You really love me that much?" Rio couldn't believe Bonita had a million dollars and trusted him with the safe combination. He looked over at her in disbelief. He'd done some horrible things for a lot less than a million.

"Yeah," Bonita responded.

"So that's why you out here carrying guns and shit." Rio laughed. Remember that day somebody started shooting at us? I was shocked as hell when you pulled out yo' gun and started bustin' back at they ass."

"I'm just paranoid. I wanna get out of Detroit."

"We are, baby. In a few weeks we'll be outta here."

Rio pulled up at his place a few hours later. Bonita had dozed off during the ride. Rio looked over at her as she slept. *Damn, she really in love with me. I finally got what I thought I wanted, but am I really ready for this?* "Wake up, baby. We home," Rio said, shaking Bonita softly.

Bonita looked around as she stretched. "I can't wait to get in the bed."

"Um… baby… I need to make a run right quick. It's only gon' take an hour or two and I'll be right back." Rio looked over at Bonita.

"Where you going? I thought we was about to chill for the rest of the night."

"We are… I just gotta handle some business right quick. Go take a long bath and get ready for ya man, and I'll be right back."

"Let me find out you trying to go see another bitch, Rio." Bonita was wondering if she should have told Rio about her money, and she definitely was having second thoughts about giving him the safe combination.

"Bonita, I told you I'm not fucking around. This about money, baby."

"But I just told you we got money, Rio. What am I supposed to think?"

"You got money, Bonita. That's your money. I still got a few weeks to stack. Don't be like that, baby. You know you got me. I've been chasing you for years. I'm not going anywhere." Rio hugged Bonita tightly then kissed her forehead. "So let me go handle my business so I can hurry up and get back home to you." Rio smiled.

After a moment, Bonita smiled as well. "Okay, hurry up," she said, getting out the truck. Bo entered the house and headed straight for the bedroom. After taking off her coat and shoes, she pulled out a sexy gown to put on after a quick shower.

Bo brushed her teeth before getting in the hot shower. As the hot water trickled down her back, she thought about her relationship with Rio and the information she'd just disclosed to him. *Lord, please don't let me get played. Please let him love me like I love him,* she silently prayed.

After showering and dressing for bed, Bonita decided to make herself a cup of tea while waiting on Rio to get back home. She headed down to the kitchen and pulled out the teabags then looked under the cabinet for a pot to boil water in. Grabbing a small pot that was inside a larger one, Bonita spotted the silencer she'd hidden.

"That's where I hid it at!" she shouted, instantly remembering the day she rushed to hide the silencer from Rio. "Fuck! Krys diary!" Forgetting all about the tea, Bonita ran to the bedroom and jumped in bed. She grabbed the diary from her purse and flipped it open to a random page and began reading.

June 20, 2006

I can't believe this bull shit! After obsessing about this nigga for a year I finally meet him. Then I get the dick and it's wack as hell!! I shoulda knew something was fucked up about that nigga, Julius Wright. Nigga shoulda been named Julius Wrong! He looks like a taller version of Jim Jones, pushing a brand new convertible Corvette—black on black... stays fresh to death and wearing enough jewelry to pond for the purchase of a house worth at least $200,000. A nigga shouldn't have all that and not possess at least six inches. Damn, this nigga coulda got away with five inches with some thickness to it. I can't believe this paid ass, sexy muthafucka got a two and a half, maybe three inch dick! And he can't even work that little muthafucka! And to think... I put on my sexy ass GiGi Hunter dress—with no underwear of course. It started off good. He pulled up in the Vette with the top down looking good as hell! I strutted my ass out to the car like I owned it, because I knew after putting it on him I would eventually be pushing that ride. As soon as I got in the car this nigga had the nerve to look me up and down then rub my thigh before sticking his hand under my dress. When he realized I wasn't wearing any panties, he stuck his finger deep into my pussy. After finger fucking me for a second he pulled his finger out and lifted it to his nose, inhaling deeply before sticking the finger in his mouth. That shit turned me on so much I told him to bypass dinner and all the formalities and head straight to the room. And this nigga wasn't cheap! He pulled up at the Ritz Carlton in Dearborn and paid for the Executive Suite in cash. I was so impressed with his swag. He wore True Religion jeans with a designer button up. His Detroit hat was cocked slightly to the left, and his shoes was so expensive, even I didn't know what they were. I should have got a clue when the elevator doors shut and he attacked me, his kiss was so foul it wet my entire face, leaving a stinking odor behind. As soon as we got in the room I had to go in the bathroom and wash my face to get the smell—that was beginning to make me sick to my stomach—off. When I came out the bathroom, this nigga had the nerve to be lying across the bed in his boxers, posted up like he was Tony Montana or somebody! Against my better judgment, I pulled the strings tied around my neck, letting my dress hit the floor then slowly sashayed over to him. Yeah... he ate the pussy like a pro... I'll give him that. But when he lifted my legs up on his shoulders I braced my self for what was to come. After a few seconds, I slowly opened one eye and saw Julius' face screwed up like he was in ecstasy. He was grunting and pumping and moaning all at the same time, but I wasn't feeling nothing. I opened my other eye and tried to look down at what he was working with, but I couldn't see anything. I rolled my hips to meet his thrust, causing him to pop out of me. I reached down to put him back in and couldn't believe what I held in my hand. I had to see the little *muthafucka to believe it, so I pulled my legs down, while suggesting we do it doggie style. I could not believe my eyes... this nigga dick was the size of a three-year-old's dick. This nigga had the nerve to say, "Um. Naw, baby... I don't like it like that." When I insisted, he got behind me and tried to stick it in, but every time he pulled back it popped out, because he wasn't even long enough to get a short stroke going! We ended up doing it missionary style and he came in less than a minute. If he hadn't given me a thousand to go shopping with tomorrow I would put his ass on blast. Sorry dick mutha fucka. I just can't understand how God would waste a perfectly good eight inch dick on a sorry ass loser like Jerome, and give Julius the dick of a child. Long story short... I won't be wasting my time fucking Julius' little dick again. I'd rather get stuck with the bill fucking with Jerome... at least he'll fuck me real good after I feed him and get him some Martell and weed.*

Bonita laughed at the memory. *Krys was so pissed off about Julius,* she thought, reminiscing. Just as Bonita was about to turn the page, she heard the door open. Naturally paranoid, Bonita quickly stuffed the diary under the mattress.

"Rio?" she called out.

"Yeah," he answered.

"I was just making sure that was you."

"Who the hell else it's gon' be?" Rio chuckled, entering the room.

"Where did you go, Rio?" Bo asked with a serious expression on her face.

"You don't trust me? How you gon' move outta town with somebody you don't even trust?" Rio answered her question with a question.

"If I didn't trust you I wouldn't have told you about the money, Rio. You know I trust you. You're the one running in and out at all times of night and being all secretive and shit."

"What! I know you not talking about being secretive! Bonita, you walking around with pistols and shit… disappear for hours at a time… and I'm being secretive?"

"Just answer the question. Where were you at?"

"Q asked me to grab something for him." Rio began undressing as he spoke.

"You couldn't do that tomorrow?" Bonita scanned Rio's body as he undressed.

"What… you wanna smell my dick?" Rio asked, holding his dick in his hand. He was hoping Bonita wasn't that kind of woman. If she was, she wasn't the woman for him after all.

"Hell naw… I don't wanna smell yo' dick!" Bonita said, insulted. "What the fuck I look like? I just asked you a fucking question."

"And I answered the question, baby," Rio said, jumping on the bed and wrapping his arms around Bonita. He was butt naked and still cold from his late night mission. "Get under the covers." Rio pulled the covers back and slid under them, making sure to put them over Bonita as well. "Come on, baby," Rio said when he noticed Bonita was pulling away from him. "It's Valentines Day and I did my part. I bought you jewelry… took you out to dinner… I even took you out for drinks." Rio smiled at the pissed off expression on Bonita's face.

"Nigga! You did not take me out for drinks! You can't count Q's house as going out for drinks." Bonita was unsuccessful at keeping her distance as Rio snuggled up under her.

"Why can't I? You had a drink… right?" Rio looked up at Bonita with puppy dog eyes. "Baby, don't play me like this on Valentines Day. I did my part… now I want some head and some pussy right now!" Rio said, raising his voice.

Bonita looked at Rio like he had lost his mind.

"I'm just playing," he quickly added. "But I do want some of this," he said, rubbing Bonita's crotch. He grabbed her hand and placed it on his hard dick. "You want some of that?" he asked, looking in her eyes.

"You know I do," Bonita said, forgetting all about her original question. She quickly undressed then stuck her head under the covers with her ass in Rio's face.

Rio playfully licked her ass. "You know I love you... right, Bonita."

Bonita twisted her body so she could look at Rio. "I love you too. Let me show you how much," she said then devoured his entire dick.

CHAPTER 16

Bo laughed. Nothing could piss her off, because soon as the weekend hit her and Rio would be on their way to Arizona. She'd already had her house emptied and donated all the furniture to charity. The only things she kept were her wardrobe and computer. She planned on destroying the computer and her work phone once she got to Arizona. Everything from her past, with the exception of Rio, would remain in the D.

The weekend couldn't come soon enough for Bo. She kept having eerie thoughts of something bad happening right before they left. She was more than ready to leave. She'd already sold her Benz and stacked that money with her already overflowing stash. Rio rented a U-Haul with a hitch to pull his truck and they were planning to pull out on Friday morning.

For some strange reason, Ray had been on Bonita's mind a lot lately. She knew once she left Detroit she would have to cut all ties with him, and her conversations with him would really be missed. In another lifetime he would have been a great guy for her. She decided to quit putting off the inevitable and give him a call.

"What's up, pretty?" Ray answered with excitement in his voice.

"What's up with you?"

"Getting ready to fight for my life," Ray responded. He grabbed his wallet, checking to make sure his badge was still there, a habit he'd formed years ago.

"You be safe. It's some psychos in the D." *Hell, I'm one of them,* Bonita thought.

"You ain't never lied. All I can do is pray. What you got going on today?" Ray secured his gun and grabbed his hat then headed toward the door.

"Not much... probably just hang out around the house." Bonita strained her ear to see if Rio was calling her. Hearing nothing, she continued to talk. "I think I feel like cooking dinner."

"Whaaaat! Not you. I rarely hear you talk about cooking anything. What you trying to cook?" Ray paused at the door to finish the conversation. He never left the house while talking on the phone. He knew it was a distraction that could get him killed.

"I don't know... maybe some Hamburger Helper Double Cheeseburger Macaroni. Something simple though." Bonita headed to the kitchen and began looking through the cabinets.

Ray laughed. "Well good luck. I'm about to head out to work, so I'll call you tomorrow."

"Okay. Be safe... and don't be fuckin' with niggas for smoking weed," she joked.

"You crazy... I'll talk to you later." Ray headed out to his car with a smile on his face.

Bonita found the Hamburger Helper and began throwing it together. Moments later, she looked up to find Rio staring at her from the entryway. He wore a scowl on his face, his braids fuzzy and in need of a redo. His oversized sweatpants hung low, showing the top half of his plaid boxers. Sweat drenched his bare chest.

"Baby... I feel sick as hell. I been shitting like this for two days. We ain't got no Vernors?" Rio raked his fingers through his frizzy braids.

"Yeah, we got some cans. You want it warm or cold?"

"I think I better drink a warm one first. What you cooking?"

Bonita held up the Hamburger Helper box then grabbed a pop from the pantry. "Take a warm shower and change your clothes. You need to put a shirt on, too."

"I'm hot as hell. Then I get cold as hell. This shit crazy!" Rio said, frustrated.

"Everybody get sick, baby. That's what I'm here for. I'll bring you some soup up once you get out the shower. I'ma rub some Vicks on your chest, too. Here, take this cough medicine." Bo handed Rio two pills.

"Thank you, baby... I would kiss you but I don't wanna get you sick." Rio retreated to the bedroom.

A few minutes later, Bonita could hear him going in the bathroom and starting the shower. She put a can of chicken noodle soup on to warm then finished up dinner. It seemed so peaceful since she'd turned off her business phone. Her personal cell phone rarely rang unless it was Rio, Ray, Q and periodically, Chris calling to plea his case. Once the soup was warm, Bonita took a bowl up to Rio.

Rio was resting comfortably in bed, sinking in a sea of down feather pillows while watching ESPN. "Thank you," he said, grabbing the bowl and sitting up to eat. The shower did him some good and he actually felt a little better.

"Let me know if you need anything else."

"Where you going?" Rio stopped eating and looked up at Bonita.

"No where. I'm just going back in the kitchen to get something to eat."

"Then you coming back in here to eat?" Rio asked then resumed eating.

"Why? What's up, baby?" Bonita said, flopping down on the bed. Rio had been acting a little strange lately, and she was curious to know what was on his mind.

Rio wanted a fresh start with Bonita in Arizona. He'd been debating if he should come clean and tell her about his secret life, but could never seem to find the right words to start the conversation. He was hoping he could find the courage to tell her before they left, but they were leaving in three days and he still hadn't said a word. "Um... I just... I just wanted to talk to you," Rio stammered.

"About what?" Bonita lay on her stomach, propped up on her elbows.

"You talked to Q?" Rio asked, stalling. He wasn't ready to come clean just yet.

"Not in a few weeks... why... what's up?" Hearing Q's name made Bonita nervous for some reason. She wasn't sure what he might tell Rio to prevent them from being together.

"Did you tell him when we were going to Arizona?"

"No... did you?" Bonita quickly asked.

"No... I kinda just wanna get ghost. I figure I can tell the fam where I'm at once I get settled." Rio finished the soup and put the bowl on the nightstand.

"I can understand that," Bonita said, getting up and grabbing Rio's bowl.

"This that nigga right now," Rio looked at his phone then said.

"I'll be back." *Please don't fuck my shit up, Q. Just three more days and we out*, Bonita thought as she entered the kitchen. She was surprised when her cell phone began ringing and she looked to see it was Q. "What's up, Q?" she casually answered.

"You," he answered. "What... you dodging me out now?" Q said in a joking manner.

"Naw... you know you always gon' be fam, Q." Bonita filled a bowl with Hamburger Helper then poured a tall glass of blue Kool-Aid with lemons in it.

"That's what I'm tryna hear." An awkward silence took over momentarily. "Um... hey... I got one more job I need you to handle for me. I promise I won't come at you like this no more. This the last one... for real," Q said convincingly.

"Q... seriously... that's not me anymore."

Q laughed. "What you mean, 'that's not me anymore?' I'm asking my fam for one last favor. After this... it's to the grave. You feel me?"

"After this it's to the grave? Naw, nigga... it's to the grave now, Q. I'm not fucking with that shit," Bonita said sternly. "Who it is... what happened... how much you paying... none of that matters to me anymore."

"But, Bo... this one is gonna be so easy... like taking candy from a baby. See—"

"Q! You not hearing me! No! I hate I ever let you talk me into this shit! I gotta live with myself knowing what I've been doing! You don't have no blood on your hands! I'm not even trying to hear that shit!" Bonita got emotion and tears began to fall.

"Oh... you not even gon' listen to what the fuck I'm trying to say? You know what... fuck it... have it yo' way. I ain't did shit but have yo' back since yo' people got murked. You act like I made you do something." Q was beginning to sound unstable. "You sucking Rio's dick so hard... you just saying fuck a nigga! How that nigga a feel if I tell him I sucked yo' pussy?"

"I'm not about to listen to this bull shit, Q. Don't call me with fucking threats. Don't hate because I don't want yo' ass." Bonita hung up the phone pissed off. She immediately heard Rio's phone ring. Nervous energy filled her body.

Bonita threw her food in the garbage and put the bowl in the sink. Her appetite was ruined. She stood around in the kitchen, stalling. Not knowing what Q would actually tell Rio was freaking her out. After standing in the kitchen opening and closing the refrigerator for a few minutes,

Bonita slowly crept back to the room. Q was still on the phone so she sat on the bed and ear hustled.

Rio looked over at Bonita as she entered the room then continued speaking. "I hear you, man. Q, we family, dawg... it's too late for all that shit." Rio paused to listen to Q rant and rave.

"I can't do that, man... I don't know what to tell you, fam." Rio pulled the phone from his ear to look at it. "That nigga hung up on me."

Bonita looked at Rio in an attempt to read his facial expression, but she got nothing. She wouldn't have to wait long to find out what Q disclosed. Rio grabbed her hand and scooted over closer to her before speaking. He looked ever sicker than he did earlier.

"Bonita, please tell me the truth... did you and Q ever fuck around?"

Bonita thought for a moment. She didn't want to chance losing Rio, so she decided to be honest with him. "One time... at my house... he ate me out."

The sad look that covered Rio's face was breaking Bonita's heart. He looked so hurt and disappointed; Bonita wondered if this would be the end of their relationship.

"But we didn't fuck. I told him it wasn't right and made him go masturbate," Bonita quickly added.

"That's fucked up, Bonita. I asked you if you fucked with him and you said no. Why the fuck you lie to me?" Rio jumped up and began grabbing clothes and getting dressed.

"Baby, you sick. Don't leave, Rio. Just let me explain." Bonita's worse fear was quickly coming true. She could feel her heart breaking in a million pieces. She reached out and grabbed Rio as he tried to leave the room, but he roughly pushed her to the side and kept it moving.

"You lied! Ain't shit to explain!" Rio said, slamming the door behind him.

Bonita felt like she was having a nervous breakdown. She couldn't stop herself from crying hysterically. She didn't know if she should leave or wait for Rio to cool down and try to talk to him when he got back. She quickly decided to wait it out. She'd come too far to lose him now.

𝔇

Rio slammed the truck door and burned rubber getting out the driveway. He couldn't believe he let himself get so vulnerable, only to be deceived. *I really thought I was gonna marry that girl. This is some fucked up shit*, he thought as he raced to get to Q's house. *That's only the half of what you don't know about this girl, Rio. You need to come holla at yo' family and get the real...* Q's voice echoed in his mind.

Rio made it to Q's place in record time. A soon as he pulled up, Q came outside and got in the truck. Nothing was said for the first few moments. Finally, Rio broke the silence.

"I'm in love with this girl, Q. Why you ain't been told me this shit?"

"I don't know, man. I didn't think you would get serious with her. I should have known y'all was so much alike y'all would hit it off." Q pulled a pack of Newports out his pocket and lit one. He offered one to Rio then lit that one as well.

"So what else she been keeping from me?" Rio asked, unsure if he was ready to hear the answer.

"Brace ya' self for this one, man. The bitch been doing hits for me for years. She a cold-hearted killing ass bitch… do whatever she gotta do to make that dollar. How can you even trust a bitch like that?" Q threw the cigarette out the window and pulled a blunt from his inside coat pocket. He lit the blunt, took a quick hit then passed it to Rio.

"What!" Rio said loudly, choking on the blunt. It took him a few moments to compose himself before adding, "Q, you bullshitting me, man. You trying to tell me Bonita been killing niggas?" Confusion wrinkled Rio's brow.

"Nigga's in the street got you pegged as the number two hitman in the city... right?" Q grabbed the blunt and hit it.

"Yeah." Rio took a long pull from the Newport then tossed it out the window.

"So who is number one, nigga?" Q looked at Rio sideways, as if it should be obvious to him.

"That nigga Bo everybody be talking... wait a minute... nigga, you telling me that Bo is Bonita?" Rio looked like a light had just clicked on in his brain.

"One and the same, fam."

"So that's how she got all that fuckin' money. She even lied about that." Rio didn't want to believe what he was hearing, but it was all adding up. "Damn... I guess a nigga can't trust a mutha fucka," he said with disappointment written all over his face.

"Man, fuck that bitch. What you need to do is get rid of that bitch and get all that money she got stacked. It's plenty bitches out here. Bo played both of us. You know where she keeps her stash?"

Rio thought about everything Q was saying. He still couldn't believe Bonita had been lying to him all this time. *Am I overreacting... can I trust Bonita?* Rio thought. *Bonita is Bo... that's some crazy ass shit. I hear this nigga Bo got over a hundred bodies with his name on 'em. Damn, that's Bonita?*

"I'm not bullshitting, dawg. You can't trust a bitch like that. She'll fuck around and kill yo' ass for yo' stash."

"Did you fuck her, Q? I mean... she told me you ate her out, but did y'all ever fuck?" Rio didn't want to let go of the future he was planning with Bonita. He was grasping for straws... hoping there was a slight chance that Bonita was capable of being honest with him.

"Hell yeah I fucked her, dawg. When I fucked her she had a little heart-shaped patch of hair on her pussy. She told you we didn't fuck? Man, please tell me that bitch didn't say we didn't fuck?" Even Q himself wasn't sure why he was lying on Bo. In his mind, she was his... and he would rather see her dead than with someone else, especially his own cousin! He was also beginning to think she was the reason he couldn't find Krystal's diary, which he was sure he hid under the mattress.

"Damn, man. She lied about everything," Rio said, deep pain laced his words.

"That's what bitches do, dawg. Now what you gon' do about it?" Q tossed the blunt tail out the window and reached for the door handle. "I'm telling you what you need to do, Rio. Get that bitch before she gets you," he said then got out the truck and walked back in the house.

Rio sat for a moment and thought about everything Q had just said to him. *Damn, Bo is Bonita... this shit is fucking me up*, he thought. *If I would have told her where my stash is at I wonder if she would have killed me for it. But why would she tell me where her stash is at? This shit just doesn't make sense. Why didn't she just tell me? But I didn't tell her that's what I was doing... 'cause I didn't want her looking at me all crazy and shit. Maybe that's why she didn't tell me. But she lied about fucking Q, too. Fuck!* Rio headed back home with a lot on his mind. Mad, hurt, and extremely confused, he didn't know what his next move would be.

𝕯

Scared and unsure of her future with Rio, once she had cried all the tears she could, Bo grabbed Krystal's diary from under the mattress and flipped it open. She'd been reading it for two hours and knew by the dates she was getting closer to the end. Unable to contain herself, she quickly flipped through the pages until she reach the last page that was written on and began to read.

February 17, 2007

I still can't go to sleep. This is the hardest thing I've ever had to deal with in my life. For the first time ever I feel like I can't go to Bonita and get her advice. Why? Why did I have to overhear that conversation? I would have been better off had I never learned the truth. Now I feel like I have no choice but to make him do the right thing... and turn himself in. That is the right thing, right? Money will make the nicest people do even the most unheard of things. I love him with all my heart, but what he did was wrong... and he needs to pay for his sins. But how will this affect my relationship with Bonita. I hope we will continue to be sisters. I love her just as much as I would if she was my blood sister. I love her just as much as I love Quincy. Oh, well... I don't know why I'm putting off the inevitable. Now is as good a time as any. Wait... would he do anything to hurt me? I hope I'm doing the right thing. Quincy would never hurt me... he's my brother. I'm going to confront him right now. I know he loves me... he just needs to get some help. Something has to be wrong with him.

Bo's mind raced as she flipped back a couple of pages and began reading the prior day's entry. She didn't even want to verbalize what she was thinking, because the thought alone was breaking her heart all over again.

February 16, 2007

I can't go to sleep. What has Quincy done now? I can't save him this time. He's put me in a fucked up predicament. Today when I went over to my grandma's house to grab some more of my things to take back to the apartment I'd left my cell phone in the car, so I picked up the phone in my old room to make a call. I wasn't aware Quincy was using the phone, and when I first heard his voice I started to hang up right away. But then he said something that will probably change my life forever. I'm ashamed to even write it down, but I can't keep it bottled up inside of me. I don't know who Quincy was talking to, but he was telling them about a day in our life that I will never forget. The day Bonita's parents were murdered by an intruder. Or so we thought... I always wondered how Quincy got to Bonita's house so quickly. I looked up... and he was there. Well now I know it's because he was always there. He was the last person to see Bonita's parents alive... because he killed them. I sat on the phone as quiet as I could be and listened to Quincy tell someone how he was the person who killed Dale and Janice. He explained how he was tired of making hundreds while Dale was making thousands. He'd asked Dale for a more important role, but Dale told him he wasn't ready yet. Quincy said he was only going to rob them, but when he walked in the house with the gun out, Janice pulled a gun from her pocket, so he had to shoot her. Dale heard the shots and ran to see what was going on. When he saw his wife shot dead on the dining room floor, he ran to get his gun from the basement, but Quincy shot him in the back before he could make it. All this and he only ended up getting a few guns, some drugs and $50,000. Quincy killed the only people who ever treated him like a son. He killed my best friend's mother and father and I don't know what I'm supposed to do. If I tell Bonita this she will hate me... I mean... he's my brother. How could Quincy do something like this? I have to do something... I can't just keep this a secret. I think I'm going to confront Quincy before telling Bonita. He needs to own up to this. What the fuck! This is the craziest shit I ever had to deal with in my life. It's eating me up to keep this from Bonita. What should I do?

Bo dropped the diary and sat in silence. Her tears flowed at a steady pace as she realized not only what happened to her parents, but also what she had to do to avenge their deaths. Frozen in disbelief, Bo sat and thought about everything she could remember from the day she found her parents murdered to the current date.

After sitting for what seemed like minutes but was actually hours, Bo stuffed the diary back under the mattress then got up and began getting dressed. She wore all black for this job, to mourn the loss of her parents, Krystal and Q. *I wonder if Rio knew anything about this,* she thought. *My gut is telling me he has nothing to do with it. Q is one crazy mutha fucka... he killed his own sister! I can't believe this nigga Q killed my family and been in my face every since. God, I swear this will be the last time.*

EPILOGUE

Rio quietly entered the dark house with his weapon drawn. Still nursing second thoughts about what he was getting ready to do, he tried to focus on the hurt Bonita had caused him. In his mind she'd been playing him all along, but the nagging question he couldn't seem to answer was why? *What is she getting out of playing me? She don't need me for anything. What if she really does love me and Quincy is just jealous and lying?* Rio couldn't get these questions out his mind.

The entire ride to his house he'd gone over different ways he could handle the situation. His first mind was telling him to pick up Bonita and leave for Arizona at that moment... in other words, to follow his heart. His pride won out in the end and led him to his current state.

As he made his way through the house, he spotted the light on in the bedroom. Rio lowered his gun to his side then took a deep breath and exhaled before walking toward the light. Once he got closer, he could see Bonita checking the clip in her gun. She was wearing all black and looked to him as if she was in the midst of a job herself. A seriously pained expression covered her face.

Bo jumped, jamming the clip back into her gun. "You scared me!" she said once she saw it was Rio entering the room. "Rio, we gotta talk, baby. I don't even know where to start." Bo sat her gun on the nightstand and began to walk over to Rio with her arms open wide. She needed to feel his arms around her and wanted him to tell her everything was gonna be all right.

Rio was conflicted. His heart raced as if it was going to give out at any minute. Thoughts bombarded his mind faster than he could process them. Bonita was just a foot or two away from him when he raised his gun. Her pained expression changed to pure horror then ultimately to confusion.

"Rio, why—" started the beginning of a question Bo would never get a chance to finish nor hear an answer to.

Rio knew if he waited a second longer he wouldn't be able to go through with it. Initially, he couldn't make himself aim for her head, so he shot her in the mid-section. The bullet tore into her side, grazing her spleen then exited.

Bo's jaw dropped at the realization of what was happening. She'd instantly grabbed her side before collapsing to the floor. As she lay there, she looked at her hand, now covered with her own blood, before looking up at Rio and once again asking, "Why?"

In a twisted way, Bo felt the least a murderer could do was allow their victim to die knowing exactly why they were dying. She herself had tried to offer that courtesy to everyone she'd bodied, and she didn't even know those people! Bo wasn't surprised by what was happening. She knew one day she would have to pay for all the families she'd destroyed with her actions. She understood that everyone she killed was somebody's husband, wife, brother, sister, son, daughter, mother, father or friend. She was well aware of the fact that murder was a sin punishable not only by the courts, but most importantly, by God. What surprised her was the person she saw behind the gun she was now sure would end her life.

Rio knew this wouldn't be easy, but he had been acting on pure emotion. Now that he saw Bonita lying in her blood pleading to know why he'd done this to her, he didn't know what his next move would be. He followed her eyes as she glanced over to her gun sitting on the nightstand. The pained expression on Bo's face was killing him as blood began to seep from her mouth. She tried to speak once again, but a fit of coughs prevented her from voicing her thoughts.

Rio knew he had to end this. *No matter what... nobody deserves to die like this. What the fuck have I done?* Rio thought. He couldn't look Bonita in the eyes, so he closed his for just a moment. As soon as his eyes reopened, Rio shot Bonita in the side of the head, putting her out of her misery. He hadn't even noticed he was crying until he saw his reflection in the mirror.

Rio snatched the comforter from the bed and threw it over Bonita, covering her face. He jumped into action and began gathering things he would need to dispose of her body. After dumping her body somewhere, he planned to return home and pack his and Bonita's money, then jump in the U-Haul to head out of state and start a new life where nobody knew him or his past. His final act of destruction would be setting fire to his place, in hopes of destroying all evidence and avoiding fugitive status.

Rio wrapped Bonita's body in plastic drop cloth then rolled her in a thick oriental rug he'd just picked up from being cleaned. In the darkness, he loaded her body in the back of the truck then drove a few miles to a neighborhood park. He dumped the body in a spot where it would be found quickly and rushed back to the truck.

During the ride home Rio had regrets, but he forced himself to brush the thoughts from his mind, because there was nothing he could do at this point. He glanced down at his ringing phone. It was Q again, so he ignored the call. Rio wasn't ready to talk to Q. Quite honestly, he didn't know if he could trust Q. And more and more he was beginning to think Q had bamboozled him.

After stopping at the gas station to purchase gas cans and gas, Rio quickly made his way back home. He moved in a robotic state as he took the necessary steps to cover his tracks. Rio secured the truck on the flatbed attached to the U-Haul then carried all the gasoline in the house. He made sure to pour a little gas in every room, saving the bedroom for last.

Rio couldn't help but break down as he entered the bedroom. The only evidence of a murder was the small puddle of blood at the foot of the bed and the small bullet hole in the wall, but he couldn't seem to get the image of Bonita lying dead on the floor from his head. Rio looked around, as if making sure there was no one around to witness his break down. He was crying hysterically as he poured gas on the bloodstained floor.

Walking over to Bonita's side of the bed, Rio poured gas all over her purse. He grabbed her gun from the bed and made sure it was on safety before putting it in his waistband. He reached to lift the mattress, intending to pour gas under it. *What the fuck am I doing*, he thought, releasing the mattress and pouring the gas on top of it instead. Rio grabbed a pack of matches he'd also picked up at the gas station and lit a few, allowing them to hit the gas on the bed. He rushed out the house, hopping in the U-Haul and hauling ass.

As Rio headed toward 194, he thought about all the money loaded deep inside the back of the U-Haul. They had loaded the money first, then the furniture and all their other things with the exception of his bedroom set, which he'd planned to load the day they left so it would be the last thing on and the first thing off the truck. He was richer than he'd ever been in his life, but he didn't feel happy.

"Fuck! I fucked up!" Rio said, hitting the dashboard. He looked over at the empty passenger seat, already missing Bonita's presence. But it was too late. He couldn't bring her back.

Rio turned the radio on. He needed something to take his mind off Bonita. An old school tune by Foxy Brown and Jay-Z crackled through the old, outdated speakers. *I guess Arizona is out of the question,* Rio thought. *All I would do is think about how Bonita was supposed to be there with me. I'm just gonna drive until I feel like stopping. It really don't matter where I go… I'm still gon' be by myself.* Rio shifted in his seat in an attempt to get comfortable then stared out at the horizon and the long road ahead of him.

𝔇

"Straight down that hallway and to the right," the funeral director pointed Chris toward the room that held Bonita's body.

"Thank you very much," Chris responded before slowly heading to the room.

Upon entering, Chris noticed the pale pink casket surrounded by pink and white flowers of every kind. The red bleeding heart he'd sent stood out among the sea of pink and white. "I guess I didn't get the memo," Chris said out loud, trying to make light of the situation by humoring himself.

He walked up to the casket and looked down at Bonita. "I can't believe this… you're really gone," Chris said, touching Bonita's cheek lightly then bending over to kiss her cold lips. "And Q was actually nice enough to tell me about the memorial he'd arranged. I'm sorry this happened to you, Bonita. My beautiful Bonita," Chris said then exhaled. "This wouldn't have happened if you were with me. I tried to tell you about the company you kept. Damn, Bonita." Chris shook his head from side to side, still not believing she was gone. "This is unbelievable." Chris swiftly made his exit, shaking his head all the way to his car.

No this mutha fucka Chris did not just come in here kissing on me and still talking shit! If I wasn't dead I woulda cursed his stupid ass out. What the fuck did he even come here for? I wish I could have sat up in this casket and told him what I really thought. I can't believe the nerve of that nigga! And Q paid for this pink ass funeral... we'll he just ought of paid for everything... it's the least he could do... seeing that he's the reason I'm lying in this fuckin' casket and not chillin' in Arizona with Rio! I guess this was his last chance to further humiliate me, because who is really going to come to my funeral? Rio was really the only person I had in my life and that nigga killed me.

Ray entered the room and headed up to the casket. He was visibly upset, his face soaked with tears. "Who did this to you!? I will not let your murder go unsolved like your friend's did, Bonita. I promise you... I'ma find the nigga who did this to you and... and... I'ma find 'em, Bonita." Ray was overwhelmed with grief. Although he and Bonita never ended up having a physical relationship, he cherished their friendship none the less.

Damn, Ray. I'ma really miss talking to you. Ironically, I guess you ended up being the only real friend I ever had. Find the nigga responsible for my death and you'll find the nigga responsible for Krystal and my parent's deaths. Even though Rio pulled the trigger, I know it was Q's manipulation that caused all this.

Ray grabbed the Kleenex he knew he'd need from his pocket and wiped his face then blew his nose with it. He looked down at Bonita's face. She didn't look like she was at peace. She looked more like she was deep in thought while resting her eyes. "We had over 400 murders in Detroit last year. Seventy percent of those are still unsolved. We're known as the place you go to get away with murder. You didn't deserve this, Bonita." Ray rubbed his hand across her knuckles. "I promise you I'm going to find whoever did this." Ray turned and walked back up the isle leading to the door.

Ray, wait! Don't go yet! Stay with me for a little while! Why didn't I follow my first mind and not get close to anyone! I fucked up! My life is over! It's like I'm just realizing I'm fuckin' dead! I'm about to be buried! Oh, God please forgive me for all my sins... please! No the fuck this nigga Q is not walking up in here. I hate you! I hope you get your head blown off when you walk out of here!

Q took his time walking up to the casket. It wasn't the first time he had to face someone he loved but had also caused their death. But this time around he was actually *in love* with the person as well. He walked up the casket and bent down, his lips lingering on Bonita's for a few seconds.

I wish I could choke the shit out of you right now! Get the fuck off me you hatin' ass nigga!

Q quivered... his heart starting beating faster as he looked around the room. He knew he was alone, but for some reason it felt like someone else was in the room. He scanned the room, glancing at all the flowers he'd sent. He figured it was the least he could do.

"Look, Bo... I know you're probably pissed off at me, but I tried everything I could to prevent this from happening. You just didn't want to listen to me! I knew I should have burned that damn diary a long time ago, but every time I tried... I just couldn't do it. It was the last piece of my sister I had left. I loved Krystal... I... I didn't want to kill her. What the fuck made that nigga Chris worthy of your time?" Q said, quickly changing the subject. "And Rio... I'm not even gon' go there. You see how much that nigga gave a fuck about you. I ain't seen that nigga since the night he killed you. He ain't even stop by to throw a nigga a stack or two before he left. I ain't surprised though; niggas ain't shit when it comes to some money." Q lowered his voice and continued. "I loved your parents. Really, I did."

Fuck you, Q! Fuck you, nigga. You didn't love my parents, Krystal or me! You're a sick, crazy mutha fucka and I hate you!

"I wasn't going there to kill them that day... I swear, Bo. I need some extra money... you know, to trick off that weekend. I figured I would just go in there and hit your father's stash he kept in the basement then sneak right back out... with your mother not seeing me. I don't know why I even had my gun out... your mother pulled a gun on me... I had to shoot her. Once I shot her and realized your father was home... I knew I had to kill him, too. I didn't even get anything until I had you go pack yo' shit, Bo." Q grabbed Bo's hand and looked at her as if she could hear every word he spoke—little did he know she could.

I wish this nigga could hear me. Damn, I wish I could kill his ass. This nigga got a lotta balls coming in here confessing like he's trying to get shit off his chest.

"Krystal wanted me to turn myself in to the police. She should have just stayed out of it. I don't know how she found out, but she confronted me... talking about if I didn't do the right thing and confess then she would tell on me. I couldn't let her snitch on me, Bo. You know I couldn't do that. I... I... had to kill her." Q finally broke down in tears. For the first time, he heard himself admit to killing his sister, and the realization of it all hurt him to his core.

"Are you okay?" the funeral director stuck her head in the door and asked. "There's some Kleenex right here." She pointed to a table in the back of the room.

"I'm good. I just need a few more minutes," Q responded between sobs. He waited until she left before continuing. "I loved all of you... your parents, Krystal, you... I loved you, Bo. Why didn't you just fuck with me? Why you let Rio come in the picture and fuck up where we was going? I'ma get out of here. I can't make it to the funeral tomorrow... I feel like I'm losing my mind, Bo. I'm sorry for everything... all the pain I caused you. I really am sorry." Quincy left the funeral home in tears.

So I guess that was it. This is so scary... not knowing what's going to happen next. This can't be hell... I would be burning if I was in hell... right? I guess I don't have any choice but to lay here and wait it out to see what happens next. This is torture... having these thoughts but not being able to speak them... not being able to move.

Just as the funeral home was preparing to close for the night, the director heard the door chimes. She looked out her office to see a tall, black man making his way down the hall toward the viewing rooms. *Wow, only four visits all day. That's really sad,* she thought as she continued to do paperwork.

He came! I can't believe he came! And he looks good, too. Damn he looks good. It's only been a week since I last saw him though, so I guess he would look the same. Now what could he possibly have to say to me?

Rio entered the room and turned to the right, opting to walk around the parameter of the room as opposed to up the center isle leading to the casket. He stopped to smell the flowers and read the cards on many of them, the majority from Q. When he finally reached the casket, he looked down at Bonita and smiled.

No this nigga ain't smiling!

"Even in death you look beautiful. I am sooo sorry, baby. I fucked up... Q played me... I just know he did. Once I realized it... it was too late. If I could take it all back I would... you have to believe me!" Rio said, touching Bonita's hand. He snatched his hand back quickly, the coldness of Bonita's hand freaking him out. He stepped back from the casket a little. "We could have had it all… and I fucked that up. I cheated myself out of happiness and all the money in the world can't buy it back for me. I'm miserable without you, Bonita. Everything reminds me of you. I can't get you off my mind. I called every funeral home I could think of everyday since I left… hoping I would at least get a chance to see you one last time. So many times I wanted to come clean and just tell you what I was doing… I now know there were times when you would look at me and want to do the same. I wish we would have just talked to each other. I really do. I know nothing I say is gonna change the way things are, but I love you so much, Bonita. I wish things could have ended differently."

I love you too, Rio. I wish things were different, too. Please just stay with me for a little while longer… let me look at you for as long as I can before the casket is closed and I'm enclosed in darkness forever.

"I'm gonna stay as long as I can, baby," Rio said as if he could hear Bonita speaking to him. He grabbed a chair and pulled it up to the casket, taking a seat. Tears poured from his eyes as he sat silently and looked at Bonita. After sitting for ten more minutes, the funeral director stuck her head in the door.

"I'm about to close for the night, sir. Her funeral is tomorrow at eleven." She sympathized with Rio so she added, "I'll give you a few more minutes alone."

"Thanks," Rio looked back to face her and said.

Rio stood and put the chair back then walked up to the casket. "I hope this isn't the last time I'll see you. Bonita, please be waiting for me when I get there… wherever there is… please forgive me and be waiting. I love you." Rio hesitated before bending over to kiss Bonita's forehead. "I love you." He turned and briskly walked up the center isle toward the exit. Rio looked back at Bonita for a few moments before walking through the door and out the funeral home.

If I can... I'll be waiting for you, Rio. I promise I won't waste any more time trying to push you away from me. I will be waiting on you, baby.

Rio looked around before pulling out the parking lot. With a heavy heart, he headed right back to the airport to catch his flight, which left in exactly one hour. He hadn't packed any bags because he didn't plan on staying overnight. He was headed right back to Kansas to focus on changing his life and learning how to live again without Bonita in it.

𝔇

"What kind of person has a funeral and not one person shows up? I've never seen anything like this in my twenty-five years preaching," the reverend complained to the funeral director.

"Just be thankful you've already been paid, Reverend Clanton. I'm going to wait an hour, just in case someone is running late, before closing the casket and having them drive it over to the cemetery."

"The funeral started at eleven... its noon," he said, looking at his watch. "I'm outta here. I don't work on CP time." The reverend left the funeral home in a rush.

The funeral director had never experienced a funeral where not one person showed up... especially a funeral as nice as this one. "I guess there is a first time for everything," she said as she walked to the front to finish up some paperwork.

An hour later, Bonita's body was driven to the cemetery on Six Mile and Telegraph to be laid to rest. Not one person had bothered to show up for her funeral.

You're born alone and you die alone… so who really gives a fuck if nobody showed up to front like they cared at my funeral. I don't… fuck em all.

A MESSAGE TO THE READER

Pssst... Hey... are you pissed off about the way the book ended? I can hear you talking shit from way in Detroit! Did you want Bo and Rio to live happily ever after? First off, let me say that you're such a sucka for love, but okay... have it your way. Look at the next page to start reading the alternate ending, where Bo and Rio lives happily ever after. Uggggg... I think I just threw up in my mouth! Anyway, forget all about the epilogue you just read... act as if it wasn't even there. Okay... If you're that emotional about it just cut the damn pages out! That was just my sick, twisted imagination at work. Chapter 17 starts where chapter 16 ended. Please tell me you did not just look back at the end of chapter 16 to see how it ended. Yo' memory that damn bad! Damn! You must be smoking that good shit! LOL! Enjoy! And don't forget to email me to let me know what you thought about Murda Mitten. And before you catch me at a book signing in your state and even ask... NO THERE IS NOT GOING TO BE A SEQUEL TO THIS BOOK!!! ☺

I love you for supporting me,

Renita M. Walker
renitamwalker@rockydpublishing.com

CHAPTER 17

Rio busted in the house confused and conflicted. During the long ride home, he'd thought about everything Q told him and it just didn't add up. Even if Bonita did fuck Q, she was in love with him, and there was nothing Q could say to make him think otherwise. *I still got a lot of unanswered questions for Bonita… or Bo,* Rio thought. Unsure of what to expect, Rio pulled out his gun and headed toward the light in the bedroom.

"What the fuck!" Bo jumped, quickly putting the clip back in her gun. "Rio, you scared the shit out of me. What the fuck you got yo' gun out for?" The look in Rio's eyes just didn't sit right with Bo, so she held on to her gun, inconspicuously taking the safety off.

"What the fuck is going on… Bo. Q told me everything. I just wanna know why you didn't just be honest with me?" Rio continued to hold his gun on Bo, not missing the fact that she'd taken the safety off her gun.

"Rio, Q is crazy! He killed my parents and Krys. I just—"

"Stop fuckin' lying!" Rio cocked his gun. "I can't believe Q was right about you." Rio knew what had to be done, but he couldn't force himself to pull the trigger.

"Rio, please… listen to me. I took Krystal's diary from Q's house on Valentine's Day. I just finished reading it and found out Q killed my parents. I think he killed Krystal too, because her last entry said she was going to confront him about my parent's murder… its right here… under the mattress." Bo was about to lift the mattress to grab the diary but Rio stopped her.

"Just stop it, Bo. That is your alias, right. You killed more niggas than most hitmen in the D your first year and a half in the game. You must be very good at manipulating mufuckas. Yo' name rings bells in the city. I felt my money slack off right around the time you got in the game. So, stop... don't fuckin' move or I'ma blow yo' fuckin' brains out. Now drop yo' gun, Bo. And let me tell you... you'll never get a chance to raise your gun."

"I can't do that, Rio." Tears escaped Bo's eyes. "Rio please... please... just listen to me. I swear I'm the one telling the truth. Q is just jealous of you because he wants me. I'm not lying to you... I love you, Rio. Q just wants you to kill me because if he can't have me he doesn't want anyone else to have me. He killed Krys, Rio!"

Bonita's phone rang, adding to the intenseness of the moment. "Can I please just answer that, Rio? It's Q calling," Bonita said. She knew it was Q by the ringtone.

Rio nodded his head, "Go ahead. Put the speaker on." He was curious to know what the fuck Q was calling Bonita for.

Bonita carefully reached over to grab her cell phone from the nightstand. "Hello," she said, hitting the speaker button.

"Umm... Bo... you by yo' self? Did Rio make it back yet?" Q asked, hoping he wasn't too late.

"Yeah... I'm alone. What's up, Q." Bo tried her best to act like nothing was wrong. This was her only hope to make Rio believe her over Q.

"What you doing?"

"I'm packing, Q. I'm leaving with Rio. I'm in love with him." Bo looked into Rio's eyes, hoping for a hit that he was changing his mind about killing her. She didn't see any change.

"Look, Rio is on his way back there to kill you. That's who do my hits I don't send yo' way. Anyway... I love you,

Bo. I still love you. Fuck that nigga, Rio. Knock that nigga off and you and me can get the fuck outta the D. I can't live without you. I... I'm a little obsessed with you," Q said in a rushed tone.

"Ya, think." Bo looked over at Rio again. This time she saw a different look in Rio's eyes.

"But in a good way. I'd never cheat on you... or do you wrong, Bo."

"Q... I read Krys' diary." A tear escaped Bo's eye. "I read every word, and I know what you did! You're lucky I'm not on my way over there to kill yo' ass! I'm finished with all that though. I can't believe I let you turn me into a monster. I'm leaving the D and starting a new life. If you sent Rio back here to kill me... for whatever lies you told him... I won't be here when he gets here. You may have succeeded in taking the man I love from my life, but I'll never be with you, Q. Never!" Bo's tears now flowed freely.

"Don't cry, baby. I promise if you just give me a chance I'll make it all better. That night you let me eat you out... that felt good didn't it? Wait til' you actually feel the dick inside you, baby. Listen to me, Bo. Kill that nigga when he gets back. Get yo' stash and Rio's and get outta there. Come here... I'll be waiting on you. I love you, Bo. I hope you make the right choice."

"You killed my mother and father, Q!!! I read the fuckin' diary! You killed Krys 'cause she wanted you to turn yourself in when she found out you killed them!"

The shock Rio felt was apparent by his facial expression as he finally took in Bonita's accusations. He was about to say something, but Bonita put her finger to her mouth then motioned for him to come to her. Rio dropped the gun to his side and walked over to Bonita. As soon as he was within reach, Bonita grabbed him up into a tight hug. The warmth of her body felt good. Rio exhaled a sigh of relief, realizing he had just been saved from the mistake he was about to make. He had already envisioned himself killing Bonita then wrapping her body in a plastic drop cloth and dumping it in some desolate park before burning his place to the ground to cover his tracks.

"Bo... let me explain. I only did what I had to do. It's not how it looks," Q said.

Bonita hung up the call. "Please tell me you believe me now, Rio."

"I'm so sorry, Bonita. I'm so sorry. I can't believe Q killed Krystal. Wait a minute... wait a minute... Q killed Krystal? He killed your parents? You read this in Krystal's diary?" Rio was still trying to grasp what was happening.

"Yes. It's all in Krystal's diary. I hate him, Rio. Q ruined my life."

"He was about to ruin mine, too. I got a plan though. We need to get the bedroom set on the U-Haul... if you still want me to go with you we're leaving tonight," Rio said. His eyes held a look of desperation. He was hoping Bonita could forgive him for almost killing her.

Bo smiled a sinister smile. "What's your plan, baby? I'm in."

After loading the few remaining things from the house into the U-Haul and putting his truck on the flatbed, Rio locked the keys in the house as he'd told the landlord he would do and headed for I94. As they rode, Bonita read the last few pages from Krystal's diary to Rio. She glanced over at him and could see the pained expression on his face as she continued to read.

Once she'd finished reading, Bo asked Rio, "Can I ask you something I've always wondered about?"

"What?"

"When we went to that wedding... I was supposed to do that hit... did you kill the groom that day?" Bo finally went ahead and asked.

"Yeah... I came right back to get you so we could leave. I was gonna make up an excuse, but you were gone. We're you supposed to do that hit?"

"Yeah, it was set up a long time before the wedding by—"

"The bride's father," Rio finished her sentence.

"Yeah! Damn... he must have really wanted his daughter not to marry that guy. Rio, you sure you don't want to just got to Arizona and try to forget any of this ever happened?"

Rio looked over at Bo and promptly stated, "After Krystal died, I promised you I was gonna find out who killed her and I would handle it... I have every intention of keeping that promise."

"I'm with you either way, Rio. I just wanted to say it so you would know I'm okay with whatever you decide to do. I love you, baby." Bo rubbed Rio's arm as she spoke.

"I love you, too, Bonita. Don't worry... after this we will be in another state starting a new life." Rio tried his best to smile at Bonita, but a crooked, half-smile was all he could manage to muster up under the circumstances.

Once they pulled up at Q's house, Rio parked the truck a few houses down on the street. "Stay here and I'll be right back," he kissed Bonita after saying.

"You sure you don't want me to come with you? Rio, Q is really crazy... he has some serious issues. I'm nervous," Bonita admitted.

Rio gave her a look that said *I got everything under control*. He kissed her again. "I got this. Just sit tight til' I get back."

"Okay, be careful."

Bo watched as Rio walked down to Q's house and knocked on the side door. She saw Q open the door then look up and down the street before turning around and letting Rio inside. Rio pulled the door closed.

🄳

"What up, cuz. The job is done and I'm on my way out of town. I just stopped by before I left to thank you for putting me up on game," Rio bluffed. He realized killing his first cousin wasn't going to be as easy as he originally thought.

"Well damn, nigga. You ain't bring me nothing as a parting gift? I know for a fact Bo had paper stacked." Q was disappointed to see that Bo didn't heed his warning, but he felt no remorse, because after all, he had tried to save her. He made his way back into the living room where he had been watching a game on TV.

"Nope, no parting gift... well... I guess in a sense I did bring you a parting gift."

"Well where the hell is it at, nigga? Damn all the riddles... I'm up out this bitch right behind you. I should just ride out with yo' ass." Q chuckled.

Rio's stomach turned as he contemplated his next move. Q's nonchalant behavior made him realize just how sick he really was. Rio was beginning to wish he had just followed Bonita's advice and kept on driving. But he was there now, so he felt obligated to finish the job not only for Bonita, but for Krystal as well. Before Q realized what was happening, Rio's whole demeanor changed. As he whipped out his gun, a mean mug etched his face. "I know what the fuck you did, cuz. How the hell could you kill Krystal? My cousin... our blood... nigga, yo' sister!"

Q tried not to show his discomfort as he stared down the barrel of the silencer Rio had attached to his gun.

"Nigga, put that shit up. I know you ain't let that bitch get in yo' head before you bodied her. She lying, dawg."

"Oh, I'm lying, Q?" Bo entered the house with her gun drawn. She had begun to worry about Rio and couldn't sit in the truck and wait any longer.

Unable to hide his shock, Q's eyes bucked and sweat beads began to form on his bald head. "What the fuck! You believing this bitch lie over your own flesh and blood, nigga? Rio, what's up, dawg? Pop this bitch, man!" Q's gun was under the couch cushion, but he knew he'd never make it to it.

"You're only fooling yourself, Quincy. We know what you did. You killed my parents and then you killed Krystal. Be a man and admit it before you die," Bo said bluntly.

"Bitch, shut yo' fuckin' mouth. You're lying!" Q said adamantly.

"Q, I heard what you said when you called her, man. It's over... you was gonna set me up."

Q looked defeated. He stood in the middle of the living room contemplating how he could get his gun without feeling a bullet from either of their guns. Realizing that was an impossible task, he accepted his fate. "Fuck both of y'all! You a bitch ass nigga, Rio! Fuck you! I can't believe you let a bitch come between us... we family!"

"Did Krystal say we family right before you strangled her? Did she?!" Bo shouted. She had never held so much hate in her heart as she did for Q at that moment.

Rio and Bo's eyes met as they silently communicated with each other. They directed their attention back to Q then simultaneously began filling his body with hot lead. Q hit the floor with a hard thud. He was dead before he landed.

"Walk normal when we get outside and don't look back," Rio said to Bo as he headed back to the side door.

"I already know, baby. I got you." Bo smiled and pulled the purple diary from her waistband. She wiped it off as best she could then put it under the couch for the police to find.

Rio smiled, realizing what she was doing. "Good idea... now they will know what happened to your parents and Krystal."

They walked out the house hand in hand, slowly making their way back to the truck.

"It had to be done," Rio said more to himself than Bo as they got in the truck. He pulled off slowly and headed back to the freeway.

"I'm never killing another person," Bo said out the blue. "I want to live a normal life, Rio. We have all the money we need. Let's just open up a business or something," Bo said, looking over at Rio to gauge his expression. She held no feelings about killing Q. It actually felt good to avenge her parent's and Krystal's deaths, but Bo knew killing was wrong. She only hoped it wasn't too late to change her life and receive God's forgiveness. She was a firm believer in Karma and planned on doing all the good she could do in hopes of being forgiven for her sins.

"Bonita," Rio said in a serious tone. "Let's just go to Africa." Rio burst out laughing. He couldn't even keep a straight face as he stole the line from the movie *Belly*.

"I'm serious, Rio!" Bonita punched him in the arm. "I'm going to use what I read in Krys diary to help me write a book."

"I sorry, baby. I'm just messing with you 'cause you sounding like T-Boz talkin' 'bout let's just open up a business. I'm with you, baby. We both are in need of a lot of forgiveness... and we'll seek it together. We've caused a lot of pain and suffering in people's lives... it's only right we try to do some good and help a few people out from now on. From here on out it's just you and me, baby." Rio grabbed a Newport from his box and lit it up. He took a long pull then exhaled the smoke.

Bonita glanced at Rio with admiration in her eyes. "Damn you be reading my mind. I can't wait to get the hell out the *Murda Mitten.*"

Rio cracked the window to let some of the smoke out. "You won't have to wait long, baby, 'cause we out this bitch!" He looked at Bonita and puckered up his lips.

Bonita leaned over to kiss her man. At that moment, she felt like everything would eventually be all right. As long as she had Rio in her life she knew everything else would work itself out. She leaned to her right, trying to get as comfortable as possible for the long ride ahead, then closed her eyes and hoped for a safe trip and a prosperous new beginning for both her and Rio.

ACKNOWLEDGEMENTS

Thank you Jesus! At times I didn't think I would ever finish this one. For the fourth time, I'd like to thank my mom, Anita Mathes, for continuing to have my back and supporting me in whatever I do (even quitting a lucrative job at Citibank to pursue this crazy book thing!) To my two sons, Anthony O. Williams Jr. and Thurston Page Green Jr. (Yeah... they both juniors... and what... don't judge me!) I love you two more than you can comprehend. Please steer clear of these Detroit streets and do something positive with your lives! To my brother, Derick, I love you wholeheartedly and there is nothing I wouldn't do for you.

Now because this book has so much violence in it and speaks of the many murders... not just murders... but unsolved murders in the city of Detroit (70% of murders in Detroit are never solved), I have to shout out all my people who lost their lives in what we call the Murda Mitten. Robert Milton Walker JR. (Eastside), Robert Person (Eastside), Anthony (Big Tony) Williams Sr. (7 Mile), Uncle Jimmy (Downtown), David Young (Six Mile), Shawn (Click Boom) McKinney (7 Mile), Billy (Downtown), Marcus (Puritan), Labaron (Warren), Reddy Red (Detroit), Don (Schoolcraft), F.M. (Six Mile), Willie (Mooka) Powell (Six Mile), Benjamin (Chico) Shavers (Eastside), Bryant P. Jones (Eastside), Johnnie Clifford Walker III(Puritan), Clarencetta Craig (Detroit), Hawk (Plymouth) Jeremiah (Spanky) Spears (7 Mile), Scooter (Schafer). I'm sure there is someone I'm forgetting at the moment, but that's still a lot of people that were murdered in Detroit for one person to know. Something gotta change.

Now on to my friends in this crazy business we call the literary industry. Ms. Michel Moore as always I have to thank you for always having my back... no matter what! You give me the strength and courage to keep writing no matter what the haters have to say. Dennis Reed you still my boy even if you are mad at me. Always understand that everything happens for a reason. K'wan you inspire me to be a more dedicated writer and to never stop having fun. J.M. Benjamin calm down a little bit. You gon' hurt somebody! T.C. Littles keep doing you girl. Mary L. Wilson thanks for showing me how real you are. Keep St. Louis on lock. Victor L. Martin keep your head up. Your time is coming to a close and great things are ahead of you. Leo Sullivan slow down a little and catch your breath. Even bigger things are coming your way. Eyone Williams I can't wait for you to hit the bricks next month! Adrian Ox Mendez thanks for the love in New Jersey. Caleb Alexander I'm waiting for your next book! Tracy Brown my Facebook friend. Marlon Mccaulsky don't it seem like just yesterday when we signed that bogus deal? T. Stuckey the first author signed to RDP. Thanks to all the bookstores that welcome me for signings. Black Visions in St. Louis (Glen and Vanessa Ledbetter & Uncle Melvin) y'all treat me so well and I appreciate it, Hood Book Headquarters in Detroit, Philly Horizon in Philadelphia, Black & Nobel in Philadelphia, Source of Knowledge in New Jersey and I have to note the Harlem Book Fair, my favorite book event. It wouldn't be right if I didn't say thanks for the Publisher of the Year nomination from AAMBC. Keith of Marion Designs thanks for hooking up my covers.

Thanks to all my family and friends who support me… Gloria Walker, Robin Bradley, Kim Kemp, Lary Walker, Cousin Cindy, Uncle Melvin, Aunt Wilma, Aunt Carol, Aunt Dorothy, Aunt Toni, Aunt Pat, Sheila Reed, Andrea Walker, Chelsea Harper, Renita Walker, Kizzie Spencer, the Spears and Campbell families, Lisa and Orfelinda (my favorite bartenders), Toney Green and all my other aunts, uncles, cousins and friends. For those of you who haven't bought one book from me yet… or even worse, ask for free books… I just have to tell you that this is my dream, but it's not free. I've invested a lot into writing books and Rocky D Publishing and I can't afford to give it all away. Nothing is free… I have expenses, so if you really do support me… buy a fuckin' book!

Shenice Reed you are like family to me. Congrats to you and Ray and your beautiful family Santannah and Randy! And thanks for gracing the cover of this book! That's huge!!!

Last but not least, Anthony Cook, once again I have to thank you for all your help with the completion of this book. You are the best reviewer and friend a writer could ever ask for. Your keen eye and honest opinion truly makes the difference between me dropping an all right book and me dropping that fire I've consistently put out. I'm forever grateful for you.

Anyone I may have forgotten please blame it on the blunts that I'm sure have fried my brains. Anyone that knows me knows that I would never intentionally hurt someone's feelings, so write your name in here_____, and don't be mad at me!

Special thanks to the loyal fans who buy all my books and spread the word about them!!!

Available @ www.rockydpublishing.com

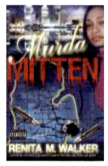
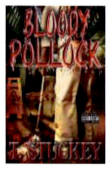

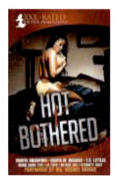

Rocky D Publishing
P.O. Box 85214
Westland, MI 48185
www.rockydpublishing.com

RDP Order Form

Name: _____

Address: _____

City/State/Zip: _____

Email: _____

Phone #: _____

Quantity	Titles	Price
	Like Night & Day – Renita M. Walker (Part 1)	$15.00
	What's Done in the Dark – Renita M. Walker (Part 2)	$15.00
	Ain't No Sunshine – Renita M. Walker (Part 3)	$15.00
	Murda Mitten – Renita M. Walker	$15.00
	Thick Like Water – Renita M. Walker (Part 1)	$15.00
	Sara & Smooth – Renita M. Walker (Part 2)	$15.00
	Bitch I'm From the D – Renita M. Walker & Various	$15.00
	Soak N Wet – Renita M. Walker & Various	$15.00
	Hot N Bothered – Renita M. Walker & Various	$15.00
	Bloody Pollock – T. Stuckey	$15.00
	Promiscuous Girl – Renita M. Walker	$15.00
	Freaky Tales – Victor L. Martin- (Kindle ebook)	$3.99

*Shipping & Handling $_____

Total $_____

FORMS OF ACCEPTED PAYMENTS:

Money Orders, Institutional Checks, Cashier Checks & Paypal, orders will take 5-7 **business** days to be delivered. **Shipping Charges are $3.95 1-2 books, $5.95 3-4 books & $1.95 for each additional book.**